A]

The Brown Sisters

Get a Life, Chloe Brown

Take a Hint, Dani Brown

Act Your Age, Eve Brown

Ravenswood

A Girl Like Her

Damaged Goods, a bonus novella

Untouchable

That Kind of Guy

Just for Him

Bad for the Boss

Undone by the Ex-Con

Sweet on the Greek

Work for It

Standalone Titles

The Roommate Risk

The Princess Trap

Guarding Temptation

Wrapped Up in You

MERRY INKMAS

A CHRISTMAS ROMANCE

TALIA HIBBERT

NIXON HOUSE

Credits: Cover Design by Natasha Snow Designs

ISBN: 978-1-913651-08-4
Published by Nixon House

Created with Vellum

For Dilip, the coolest dentist ever.
Don't ask why this book in
particular is yours; just accept it.

CONTENT NOTE

Please be aware: this story discusses topics that could trigger certain audiences, such as domestic abuse, homelessness and intrusive thoughts.

CHAPTER 1

"Here's your guy."

Bailey turned to look at Tara, who was sitting on the counter chewing a handful of mini marshmallows.

"Careful," Bailey warned. "Michael will be done cashing up soon. If he catches you nicking merchandise again—"

"Girl, did you hear me? I said he's here." Tara widened her grey eyes as she spoke around the mouthful of sweets. Then she jerked her head towards the windows at the front of the coffee shop, the ones that faced out onto the street.

Bailey had been trying to stay cool, but she couldn't resist. She looked.

The windows were covered in Christmas decals—snow, baubles, a few reindeer—and it was already dark outside. But she could still see him clearly, the streetlights glinting off of his distinctive auburn hair.

Hot Coffee Guy.

Reflexively, Bailey patted her long dreadlocks. They were shoved up into a raggedy bun and covered by a hairnet, but still—the urge to make sure that she looked presentable was instinctive. And embarrassing.

"Wonder what he'll order today?" Tara waggled her eyebrows.

"You know what he'll say," Bailey answered, trying to keep her voice light. She turned away from Tara's knowing eyes, busying herself with tidying up the mugs.

"Yep," Tara said, still chomping on marshmallows. She lowered her voice and murmured in a passable imitation of Hot Coffee Guy: "*Surprise me.*"

"Shhh," Bailey hissed as the shop's door creaked open, the little bell above it tinkling.

"Don't be so uptight. You should be happy he's here. I wish he'd flirt with *me.*"

"Oh my God, stop. It's not flirting! He's just a nice guy."

"Sure, babe," Tara laughed. But—thank God—she shut up. She even hopped off of the counter and put away the jar of marshmallows. Truly, she was a model employee.

Heart pounding—and wasn't that utterly ridiculous?—Bailey focused on the mugs. She stacked them neatly as awareness crept up on her, setting off some sixth sense she'd never known she had. At least, not until the first time he'd walked into the shop. She didn't even know his name. And yet, the moment he spoke, her body relaxed as though she'd been waiting to hear his voice.

"Hey, Bailey," he said, in that achingly low rumble.

Trying to move slowly—the last thing she wanted was to come off as eager—she turned to face him with a polite smile.

Oh, he was so fucking gorgeous.

He had both leather-gloved hands on the counter, and he was leaning towards her with his usual heart-stopping grin. Full lips + white teeth + thick stubble = Very Flustered Bailey. His dark red hair swung silkily around the sharp, masculine lines of his face, softening his aquiline nose and heavy brow. He was so tall and so broad that his leather-clad shoulders filled her view almost entirely. For a second, Bailey allowed herself to imagine those shoulders becoming her world, leaning over her in far more intimate surroundings...

Then she gave herself a mental slap and exited fantasy land.

"Hi!" she chirped. "What can I get you?"

His green eyes crinkling at the corners, he gave the same response he'd been giving her for over a month: "Surprise me."

"Alright," Bailey smiled, as though she didn't know *exactly* what she was going to give him—as though she hadn't been thinking about it all day. "We just started our Christmas specials, so it'll be something you've never had before!" God, she sounded like an ad. *Come one, come all, and enjoy the new beverages at Espresso-Go!*

“Sounds good," Hot Coffee Guy said as she grabbed a mug and switched on the electric grinder. “Christmas specials… Is that why you're wearing that jumper?"

Oh, crap. With a wince, Bailey looked down at herself.

Why, God, *why* did he have to come in on the shop’s Christmas jumper day? And why had she, carried away by festive spirit, worn a scarlet and green monstrosity with a knitted version of Rudolph's face popping out from the chest like a Christmas parody of Alien? She could hear Tara snickering in the background as she rinsed out the blenders. Tara, who had 'forgotten' her Christmas jumper and wore nothing more outrageous than an apron and a sprig of tinsel tucked into her ponytail.

Bailey squeezed her eyes shut, as if blanking out the world could somehow save her from the indignity of this moment. He wasn't supposed to come in today, damn it. He'd been in yesterday, and he never came two days in a row.

But here he was.

Pulling herself together, Bailey opened her eyes and pasted a smile on her face. "Yep!" she said brightly. "I love Christmas. It's my favourite holiday." Obviously. Because she wasn’t already uncool enough.

But he surprised her. He picked up one of the Christmas-tree-shaped chocolates on the counter with a smile and put it by the till. "Mine too," he said. And then: "I like the jumper."

Oh. Biting her lip on a smile, Bailey turned to heat up the milk. She whipped the white liquid full of air until it was hot and creamy, ignoring the way that the steam fogged up her glasses. With practiced hands, she poured the milk into a mug while her vision was still blurry, then followed it up with a shot of espresso, a squirt of gingerbread syrup, and flakes of chocolate. As she worked, her foggy lenses cleared bit by bit.

She turned to present Hot Coffee Guy with his Christmas confection. "Gingerbread cappuccino," she smiled, slightly breathless. As though she'd run a marathon instead of making a coffee. Lord, when would she stop being such a dork?

"Thanks," he said, taking the mug.

"And you want the chocolate too?"

"Yes, please. Feeling festive all of a sudden." He winked, and she thought she might drop down dead. How could one man be so bloody sexy?

As she tapped in his purchases at the till, he pulled out his wallet. "It's very impressive, by the way, how you can do that with your glasses all steamed up."

Bailey looked up sharply, mortified. *He saw?* Obviously yes, if his grin was anything to go by.

"You're like a little coffee magician," he continued.

She felt her cheeks warm up under his smoking-hot smile. He was like the sun, and she was the kid flying too close. Her mind scrambling, Bailey did the first thing that popped into her head. She grabbed a pen from beside the till, waved it around like a wand, and said "Bibbity, bobbity, boo!"

Hot Coffee Guy's lip twitched. Then he coughed. And then he burst out laughing, as though he simply couldn't hold it in.

Oh, fuck.

Bailey dropped the pen and resisted the urge to let her head fall into her hands. Behind her, she heard Tara giggling hysterically.

Why on earth had she done that?! What was wrong with her?! Did she *want* to die alone and sexless?

Clearly.

The jangle of the door's bell cut through the laughter filling the shop, and Bailey looked up, ready to tell the newcomer that the machines were going off for the night. Yes, she was prepared to be that much of a bitch right now.

But at the sight of the customer, worry filled her.

"John?" She frowned. "Are you okay?"

The laughter stopped as Tara came forward, peering at the slender man who'd just walked in. "Oh, Christ," she said. "You look bloody freezing. Let me make you a cuppa."

John shook his head, his teeth chattering. He walked up to the counter, his huge, greying backpack on his shoulders. That backpack contained all of his worldly goods, aside from those he wore. And today, he was wearing less than usual.

The tips of his ears and the end of his nose were bright red, so cold they must have been painful. He rubbed his palms together, obviously trying to warm up his hands through their thin, hole-y gloves. Bailey rushed around the counter to reach him, barely noticing that the movement brought her right past Hot Coffee Guy. She wrapped an arm around John's shaking shoulders and led him to one of the soft, worn armchairs littered around the shop. The only other customer—an older man in a fancy suit—downed the last of his coffee before stalking out with a disgusted glance. Bailey ignored the fucker.

"Where's your coat?" she asked.

John just shook his head, his usual biting humour conspicuous by its absence.

"Did someone take it?" Bailey demanded, horrified.

"No, no," he said quickly. His voice shook, his teeth clattering together. "I gave it away."

"What?! Why?"

"Saw someone who needed it," he mumbled. Tara bustled over and thrust a large mug of tea into his protesting hands, milky and sweet, just the way he liked it.

"*You* need it!" Bailey insisted. "You mustn't do that! You'll catch your death!" Conscious of her voice's hysterical tone, she took a deep breath. John didn't need her harping on at him, and she wasn't his mother. But God, homeless people actually *froze* to death in the winter. He couldn't just give away his clothing willy-nilly!

"I'm sorry to come in here," he said uncomfortably. "I don't want to cause you any more trouble. Just needed to warm up a bit."

"Don't worry," Tara said. "Michael's in the back. Drink your tea, chick."

"Cheers, Tara." He took a sip, his eyes closing.

Bailey thought fast. They needed to get John a coat, but the shops would be closing soon. He was a small man, no older than her for all his face had been ravaged by the elements, and he was always giving away what little he had to those he saw sleeping rough. They'd become friends when he started coming into Espresso-Go for the odd cup of tea—until Michael, their manager, had put a stop to that. Apparently, John's presence 'lowered the tone'.

God, Bailey could throttle that man.

A strange feeling cut through her thoughts; the sensation of being watched. She turned instinctively and found Hot Coffee Guy right where she'd left him, looking at her with something indescribable in his eyes.

"Oh, God," she said, throwing up her hands. "I forgot, I'm supposed to be ringing you up!"

"I can wait," he said. "Don't worry."

Then another male voice entered the fray, shattering any semblance of peace.

"What's going on out there?" Michael called. His bleating tones were swiftly followed by his appearance in the doorway of the back office. He had an earphone in one ear, but the other was dangling down, unused. *Crap*. Busted.

"Nothing," Tara said. She gave him a winsome smile and fingered one of the vast gold hoops in her ears, her glittery nails gleaming.

Michael's bald head gleamed too as he gave her a dour look.

"Take off those monstrosities, Tara," he said. "Health and safety, you know that." Then his habitual frown deepened into a grimace as he caught sight of John. "What is *that* doing here?" Michael demanded. "Did he pay for that drink?"

"Um..." Tara faltered.

"I'm paying for it," Bailey said. "Come on, Michael, it's the end of the day. We're about to close anyway—"

"There's a paying customer right there," Michael interrupted pompously. He gestured towards Hot Coffee Guy. "And you are neglecting him!"

"I'm fine, mate," said Hot Coffee Guy. "Let the girls sort him out, eh? He looks sick."

Michael cast a jaded glance over John's shivering figure. "Sick? More like he hasn't had a hit in a while."

"Here, now!" John surged up, suddenly finding his voice. But he was cut off as Hot Coffee Guy reached over the counter and grabbed the front of Michael's woolly Christmas jumper, dragging him forwards until their faces were inches apart.

"You better watch what you say," he murmured, his voice tense—as if he were really angry. As if he were suddenly, on account of an absolute stranger, *furious*. "People might think you're accusing him of something. And we wouldn't want that, would we?"

Michael spluttered as he was released. Straightening his jumper indignantly, he looked over to where Bailey and Tara stood gaping. "I am your manager," he stammered, "and I want *both* of these men gone from the premises!"

"But—" Bailey began.

"No more out of you Miss Cooper, or you can join them!"

Bailey's mouth worked as she struggled to find an answer. She saw Tara's worry, Michael's rage, John's humiliation. Then her gaze settled on their leather-clad defender, who was clearly incensed, his fists clenched at his sides.

And suddenly, Bailey was filled with the kind of reckless outrage that she had felt only a few times in her life.

The first time was on the day of her mother's second wedding, six months after Daddy died. Bailey had been seven. She'd shoved her fist into their four-tier wedding cake and spent the day in glorious disgrace.

The second time was at her school's prom in Year Eleven. She'd only been at that school for a year and had never managed to infiltrate any friendship groups—story of her life. So, when she saw one girl being cruelly mocked by her so-called-friends all night, she took the slight almost personally. And she *might* have helped the girl teepee her friends' limousine. But there had been no witnesses, so really, who could say?

The third time was at the hospital, two years ago, when a doctor informed them that her mother's chest infection had been a misdiagnosis; that she was actually suffering from stage four lung cancer. That night, Bailey, had... Well. She didn't like to revisit that night.

And now she was here, and her dickhead boss was giving her that smug *Got you* look, and John was getting up to leave with utter embarrassment on his face, and she was *not fucking having it.*

"Fine," she spat. "I'll go, then. Wait for me, John."

He looked over at her, something warm dawning in his eyes like the sunrise.

"*What?!*" Michael spluttered. "Do you understand what I'm saying, Bailey? I will sack you!"

"No you won't," Bailey said confidently, throwing off her little half-apron. "Because I quit."

CHAPTER 2

"Oh God, oh God, oh God, oh God."

Cash Evans watched as the cute little barista, Bailey, stamped her feet and rubbed her hands against the arms of her jumper. He couldn't blame her. It was bloody freezing outside. She chanted her shock as she stamped, staring worriedly into the window of the coffee shop.

And if he noticed the way her wide hips and full thighs bounced beneath those tight, black trousers she wore—well. That didn't make him *too* much of an arsehole, did it?

It probably did. But he couldn't bring himself to care.

"You shouldn't have done that," John was saying, rubbing his own hands together.

She took a break from her stress-chant to give the poor guy a weak smile. "Don't be silly," she breezed. It wasn't convincing. "I had to leave anyway We need to get you a coat."

"Bailey, I told you before. You can't just keep buying me things—"

Suddenly, the door to the coffee shop swung open. Tara stood there, an apologetic wince on her pretty face. Her arms were piled high with a thick coat and messenger bag, which she held out to Bailey.

"You forgot your stuff," she said loudly. And then, lowering her voice: "I'm so sorry, Bailey. I should—"

"You should go back to work," Bailey interrupted. "Before he loses it and sacks you too."

Cash stared, feeling like he'd stepped into some kind of alternate reality.

He'd been coming to buy fancy coffee from this woman on a semi-regular basis for weeks now—and truthfully, he'd had to exert a hell of a lot of control to keep it at that. No increase in visits. Certainly no asking for her number. Just harmless flirting.

Because there was no way that a woman as adorable, as sweet, and as effortlessly sexy as Bailey could be anything other than a persona. Right? It was like a character she slipped into, along with her uniform. She was just chasing tips. Taking service with a smile to the next level. It couldn't be real. She couldn't *really* be like this.

Except here she was: no apron, no job, still Bailey.

What. The. Fuck?

Cash watched as she slid her huge, puffy coat onto John's shoulders, arguing fiercely against his protests. The man was still shaking; clearly, he needed it. But it was a freezing December night, and Bailey's jumper wouldn't keep her warm for long. Cash shrugged off his leather jacket, pushing it towards her.

"You take this," he said. "Doesn't look like much, but it's warm enough."

She turned, looking up at him with eyes that glittered in the dark. Those eyes were better than a shot of espresso; especially when she stared at him like he was some kind of hero. A man could get used to that.

"What's your name?" she asked, the question startling him. "You never told me."

He grimaced. There was a reason he hadn't mentioned his name. "It's Cash."

"Really?" He waited for a smirk or some over-the-top coo that would shatter his impression of how genuine she was. But all that came was her sunny grin. "That's very… American," she said with a good-natured laugh.

Shaking his head, he put the jacket over her shoulders as she'd just done to John. "Yeah," he muttered. "That's one way of putting it." But he felt his lips curl into a smile.

"I can't take your coat," she protested. "You'll be cold."

"I'll be fine." He let his gaze rake over her face, tracing its smooth contours. Then her lips parted, and he forced himself to turn away. Because fuck, the sight of her soft mouth slightly open, just like it would be if she were gasping beneath him—

Cash had known he had a thing for the girl at the coffee shop. But it was beginning to turn into a problem.

John stood watching them, a smile playing about his bloodless lips. He was still shaking, clutching his backpack to his chest now. The longer Cash looked, the more he realised that John was just a young man, despite the weariness that clung to him like a parasite. In a split second, Cash made his decision.

"Come on," he said. "Let me take you somewhere." Because aside from anything, if he didn't start moving now, he might do or say something to Bailey that he'd eventually regret.

Before he could second-guess himself, Cash started off across the square. He didn't have to look back to know that the pair were trailing after him. Cash didn't have a lot of positive qualities, he knew that. But one thing was for sure: when he spoke, people listened.

Just a few ice cold minutes later, he led the way into a nearby hotel. He headed to the front desk and had a brief exchange with the perky young woman behind it. Just as she handed over a keycard—and Cash handed over his credit card—he felt a gentle touch at his shoulder.

He turned to find Bailey looking up at him, his leather jacket dwarfing her narrow shoulders and her delicate brow furrowed.

"What are you doing?" she asked, her voice low.

"Booking a room."

She raised her eyebrows. "Like in *Pretty Woman?*"

"I've never seen *Pretty Woman.*"

"Oh. Um... Never mind."

Cash didn't understand half of the references she made, but he definitely enjoyed the embarrassed smiles she flashed after making them. Still, he remembered, they weren't at the coffee shop now. There was no time to indulge his weird fascination with this girl.

"For John," he said shortly. "Just for a week or so. Until we can sort him out."

Her cheeks plumped as she smiled wide. And there was that look again, the one that said, *My hero.*

Not true. But he was starting to think he'd like it to be.

There you go again, lusting after treasure like a beast under a bridge.

"Here you are, Sir," said the receptionist, holding out his card with a white-toothed smile. "That's all sorted for you."

"Thanks, Mandy," he answered, reading the name on her badge. Force of habit.

He turned to catch John's eye, indicating to the younger man that he should follow. Then he headed to the lift, and they all made their way to room 302.

"Here we go," Cash said, unlocking the door and stepping into a spacious room with a tea set, double bed, TV, and ensuite. John walked in and Bailey followed, closing the door behind them.

"For... for me?" John asked, his hoarse voice barely a whisper.

"Yeah. Just for now." Cash handed the keycard over, then grabbed his wallet from the back pocket of his jeans. He pulled out a business card and put it on the side table, by the phone. "You can call me tomorrow, or I'll call you sometime after lunch. I think we could do something to help you get back on your feet."

John stared, his eyes wide and brimming with tears. Behind

him, Bailey turned tactfully away. "Why are you helping me?" the younger man asked.

Cash spoke quietly. "Because this could happen to anyone. This could happen—" his throat felt tight suddenly, but he pushed through the rising panic, mastered it, forced it back into the farthest recesses of his mind. Clearing his throat, he finished: "This could happen to me. And if it did, I'd want help. Everyone deserves help." Then he smiled, as though that could break through the heavy air that had fallen on the room. "Anyway," he said. "It's Christmas."

John reached out a hand, hope and joy and relief shining through his tired features. Cash echoed his movement, and the two men shook hands firmly before one of them—or perhaps both of them at once—pulled the other into a hug.

"Thank you," John said softly. "Thank you. One day I'll repay your kindness." The quiet words rang with the solemnity of a vow.

Cash shook his head. They pulled apart, and John made his way over to the window, gazing out at the lights of the square. While his back was turned, Cash pulled a handful of twenties from his wallet and put them at the end of the bed, along with a business card.

"We'll leave you to it, mate," he said, heading towards the door. "Get something to eat, yeah?"

John turned, surprise on his face. Then he saw the money on the bed. "Oh, Cash, no—"

"Stop it. Need you fighting fit." He winked. Then he said, "Let's go, Bailey," before he could stop himself. As if he had any control over her. As if they were a package deal. As if she'd follow.

But she did, for some reason, and that brought the ghost of a smile to his face.

"Have a good night, John," she called. "I'll ring you too."

"Bailey. Thank you. Thank you for always being so good to me."

"You don't need to thank me. You're my friend."

Cash watched as she smiled at John, her honesty shining through like a star. She was so blindingly, beautifully bright, and yet he couldn't look away. He should look away, shouldn't he?

They walked out into the corridor, shutting John's door behind them.

Cash leaned against the blandly papered wall, studying the design on the thick hotel carpet. The shades and shapes of its brash pattern were so violently unsuited that they practically offended his eyes. They definitely offended his artistic sensibilities.

"Hey," Bailey said softly. "Cash." The sound of his name on her lips sent a thrill through his core. It was like the first time he'd gotten on a motorbike, or the high after his first tattoo. But it came from nothing more extreme than this woman. Maybe it was because she was so very off-limits—so very out of his league. Maybe it was because she'd been safe when she was stuck behind a counter, but now she was real and he wanted her badly. Whatever the reason, in that moment, he made the decision to chase the feeling she gave him.

"Yeah?" he asked.

She stepped forward, and he stood up straight as though she had him on a leash. Which she did, really—only it was secured around his suddenly aching balls, and she didn't even know it yet.

"Why did you do that?" she asked, her voice solemn.

"Do what?"

"Help John."

He raised a brow. "Why did *you* help John?"

"Because I like him," she said immediately. No hesitation. "And I think he's a good guy. And I wish… I wish things were better. For everyone."

Cash tried to keep himself under control—but he'd never been very good at that. So he wasn't surprised when his hands moved, apparently of their own volition, to gently tug away the hairnet that still covered her head. "Maybe I trust your judgement," he said, his voice low.

She held perfectly still as he pulled off the hairnet, like a doe freezing just before it fled. "You don't even know me."

I wish I did. It was the truth. Just like it was true that he'd spent more than a few nights thinking of her—of her smile and her tip-tilted eyes and the way her hands moved as she poured drinks—wishing that he were a different kind of man. The kind that she deserved.

But he wasn't. He was Cash.

So he stepped away from her abruptly, doing his best to ignore the way her eyes dimmed. Then he pulled another card out of his wallet and tossed it to her like she was some kind of nuisance.

Before he could see the look on her face—the look that would shatter any illusions he had about ever being her hero—he turned away. As he stalked down the corridor, he called over his shoulder: "I've got a job for you, if you want it. Be there at ten."

She didn't say a word in reply. He imagined her standing there amongst the bland walls and the awful carpet and the countless identical doors, staring at his business card.

Then again, she might've dropped it in disgust. He had no idea. His rules were clear: Cash never looked back.

And before now, he'd never wished that he could.

CHAPTER 3

The next morning, Bailey stood outside of Fallen Tattoos, clutching Cash's card. It was black, with his name, contact details and business address printed on it in a stark white font. Something about it was… imposing.

And the facade of the shop standing before her was pretty imposing too. This was definitely the place. But God, what the fuck was she doing here?

For a moment, Bailey wavered, fiddling nervously with zip of the leather jacket slung over her arm. But then she steeled her spine and mentally pulled on her big girl knickers. After the events of last night, she really had no choice—she *needed* a job. Now.

So why look a gift horse in the mouth? Even an incredibly hot, intimidating gift horse who apparently owned a tattoo parlour?

Okay, yeah—she should leave.

But as she turned to scurry off home—not that it would be *home* much longer if she couldn't pay the bloody rent—the shop's front door opened a crack. A girl's head poked out of the gap, her short, choppy hair dyed a screaming pink. "Hey," she said. "Are you waiting for Cash?"

"Um...." Bailey faltered, her mind scrambling.

"Well, come in then," the girl said. "I'm freezing my bloody tits off here."

"Right," Bailey muttered. "Sorry." Then, because she was a pushover of epic proportions, she turned right around and marched herself into Fallen Tattoos.

Stepping out of the icy street and into the shop's cozy warmth was a treat for the senses—except for her sight, which immediately blurred as her glasses fogged up. With a sigh, Bailey waited for them to calm the hell down.

And then, when they finally did, she gaped at the magic surrounding her like a kid at a fair. Because, as dark and intimidating as Fallen seemed on the outside, inside it was a Christmas wonderland.

The room was a foyer of sorts, holding a desk along with a comfortable seating area. Every spare surface was festooned with brightly coloured tinsel, or fairy lights, or some combination of both, and a small Christmas tree stood proudly amidst the brown, leather armchairs and comfy-looking sofa at one end of the room.

The festive cheer was even more incongruous when one considered the decor beneath: the room's walls were covered in a variety of artwork, from hand-drawn tattoo designs—accompanied by photographs of the finished tattoos themselves—to bold depictions of animals, landscapes, and pop-culture motifs that were painted directly onto the wall. At various points around the room, there were framed posters exhibiting bright, cartoon-like pictures that reminded Bailey of the old-fashioned tattoos she'd see in comic books as a kid. Each image had a price beneath it, and the posters were all entitled 'Flash'.

"Wow," Bailey breathed, taking in the brilliance of the many-layered contrasts.

"It's cute, isn't it?"

Oh. Somehow, she'd managed to forget that she wasn't alone. The pink-haired girl was smiling at her from behind the desk, elbows resting against its dark surface, her striking face cupped in her hands.

"Yeah," Bailey smiled back, shifting awkwardly. "Um... Should I...?"

"Oh, yes, sit down! Cash will be here soon. He usually comes in earlier than me. I don't know what's held him up today."

Nodding, Bailey unzipped her coat and settled herself down into one of the leather armchairs. It sank comfortingly beneath her weight, like the kind of chair you'd find in an old family room—or at least, the kind of chair Bailey imagined you'd find. Her experience of family wasn't exactly traditional. But a girl could dream.

"What's your name?" the pink-haired girl asked. She had the kind of bright tone and staccato voice that young children used, full of hummingbird energy.

"Bailey. What's yours?"

"Gemma," she said. "Everyone calls me Gem."

"Ah. That's cool." In fact, everything about Gem was cool. Her short, pink hair, the silver studs through her nose and eyebrow, the countless mismatched earrings running along her earlobes. She wore a band tee cut up into a vest, and its short sleeves displayed a ton of colourful little tattoos scattered up and down her arms. There were words and phrases, symbols, fractured images—none of them seemed connected, but somehow they looked perfect together.

Gem cocked her head to one side, the movement birdlike, and Bailey realised that she'd been staring. Her cheeks heating, she stammered, "I, um, I love your hair."

"Thanks," Gem smiled, running her fingers through the choppy strands. "I like yours too."

"Oh." Bailey raised her hand self-consciously to her plain bun. She'd had no idea what to do with her hair—or her clothes, for that matter—and now here she was in an old skirt-suit that was clearly unsuitable, her hair pulled back severely. But Gem was probably referring to her locs, rather than the bun. "Thanks," Bailey said, fingering the leather of the jacket in her arms like a talisman.

Another awkward silence descended.

Looking around for some kind of conversation starter—or any sign of her brain, which she'd clearly left out on the street—Bailey's eye caught on a little table beside her. A sloppy pile of magazines was splayed over it, their covers showing scantily-clad women with porcelain, tattoo-covered skin.

Bailey chose one at random, flicking through the pages as her nerves increased. Why had Cash invited her here? He said he had work for her, and she definitely needed that—but what could she do in a place like this? She was a psychology undergrad and a part-time barista, not a tattoo artist.

Her rapidly moving fingers paused as her gaze snagged on a familiar pair of piercing green eyes. Bailey's brows shot up as she recognised the very man she was here to see, smouldering up at her from the magazine page. Cash's hair hung over his handsome face, a smirk tilting his lips. His arms were folded over his broad chest, corded with muscle and covered in ink.

Wunderkind Cash Evans Returns As Hometown Hero, the article said. Bailey zeroed in on the opening paragraph.

Cash Evans burst onto the international scene way back in 2010, and he's stayed relevant ever since through a combination of fine-artistry, innovative techniques, and global touring. Now the versatile artist is back in his home city of Nottingham, opening his own studio: *Fallen Tattoos.*

Bailey flipped to the magazine's front cover, searching out the publication date. *September 2016.* So Cash was some kind of, what —tattoo superstar?

She skimmed through the next paragraph, which described the shop, eagerly searching for more information on her enigmatic rescuer. But her focus on the magazine was interrupted by the sound of the shop's door opening. She looked up in time to see Cash himself walk in, a black crash helmet tucked under his arm.

"Morning, Gem," he said, his voice low and weary. It was a little past 10 A.M., yet he sounded like he'd just finished a day's hard labour.

"Hey," Gem said, looking up from her computer screen. "You have a visitor."

Cash followed her gaze to the seating area, a frown furrowing his brow. Bailey stood. "Hi," she said, stepping forward hesitantly. "Um... I brought your jacket."

His lip curled. The expression wasn't a smile. "Is that all?" he asked.

Bailey bit her lip. She had no idea why, but the sweet guy she knew from the coffee shop seemed to have disappeared. In his place was an intimidating bear. Perhaps the dark circles under his eyes explained his sudden attitude. He looked like he hadn't slept all night.

Yeah. That was all. He was just tired. Pushing her nerves aside, Bailey straightened her spine and forced herself to speak clearly. "That's not all," she said, her voice firm. "You mentioned last night that you could help me with... with my job situation."

Okay—was she imagining things, or had Gem's jaw just dropped? If it had, the girl regained her composure in record time. She was now tapping away at the computer as though she hadn't a care in the world.

"Yes," Cash said. He stalked towards Bailey like a tiger after its prey. She had to force herself to stand still as he loomed over her, mere inches between them now. He reached out a hand, and she held her breath as she waited for him to touch her...

Only to exhale when he took the jacket she was holding out.

"Thanks," he said wryly. The knowing gleam in his emerald eyes brought a blush to her cheeks. He turned and headed towards the far end of the room where an open doorway beckoned. "We're looking for a receptionist," he threw over his shoulder. "Come up to my office and we'll discuss the position."

After a moment of indecision, Bailey scurried after him in her sensible heels. She smiled at Gem as they passed by the desk, only to falter as she saw the expression on the other woman's face.

Gem's jaw had *definitely* dropped this time.

Oh, dear.

CHAPTER 4

Bailey kept her eyes glued to Cash as they ascended the narrow staircase—which was a mistake, because his jeans were tight and his arse was tighter, and it all made her feel slightly… warm.

Still, she followed him in self-conscious silence. He led her along the short corridor at the top of the stairs, then into a spacious office filled with cheap chairs, cheaper desks, and several thousand pounds worth of MacBooks.

"Sorry about the decor," he said, sliding into a wheeled chair behind the largest desk. It sat directly in front of a wide window and was flanked by two locked filing cabinets. "We need to get Gem to work her magic up here," he continued. "But she's so busy now."

"Right," Bailey murmured. "About Gem—"

"Hang on." He reached into a nearby drawer and produced a battered A4 notepad and an old biro. Bailey watched as he flipped through the pages, revealing snatches of darkly-shaded artwork. The glimpses were so compelling, she was drawn forward almost against her will.

But then he came to a clean page and popped the lid off of his pen, looking up at her with a professionally bland expression.

"Shop's open ten 'til five for consultations, but we only take appointments from eleven. Gem gets here about half an hour early to open up, but that will be your job from now on, too. Unless I get there first. We're open Monday to Saturday. What hours can you do?"

Bailey reached up to fiddle with one of her locs, then remembered that they were coiled neatly on top of her head. She drummed her fingers awkwardly against her collarbone instead. "Um... I can't do Mondays, or Wednesday mornings. Uni. But are you sure—?"

He looked up sharply, his frown cutting her off. "What do you mean, *uni?"* he demanded.

"University," she said slowly. "I'm an undergrad at—"

"How old are you?" He dropped the pen and folded his arms, leaning back in his chair. But the relaxed pose was at odds with his clenched jaw and the way his words were forced out from between gritted teeth.

"I'm twenty-five," she said. "Oh, no—twenty-six, actually. It was my birthday last week." She gave a little wave of her hands. "Hooray for me!"

He stared, stony-faced. God, why the hell was she so embarrassing?

"But anyway," she forged on, folding her hands safely behind her back. "What I'm trying to say is... well. I'm... I'm not taking Gem's job, am I?"

He stared at her for a moment longer. Then, suddenly, he barked out a laugh. "That's what you think? That I'd throw out my employees for the next pretty girl that comes along?"

Bailey felt her cheeks heat. "No! I mean—wait. Pretty?"

He arched a brow.

Funny; he'd been a hell of a lot more charming when she was just serving him coffee.

With a sigh, Bailey explained. "I just meant, I know you're a kind-hearted guy." Even if he appeared to have undergone a personality transplant overnight. "And if Gem is already doing this job, there's no reason for you to pay two people for the work of one."

Cash unfolded his arms and picked up his pen again. He began marking out bold, swirling lines on the corner of the notepad, not even looking down at his hands as he did so. Like it was habit. Muscle memory. His eyes remained on hers, and she felt like a fly drowning in lemonade on a hot summer's day. Doomed, and a little too happy about it.

"I appreciate your concern," he said. "But don't worry. My kind heart"—the twitch of his lips told her what he thought of *that* claim—"doesn't stop me from running my business properly."

"Oh, I didn't mean—"

"Bailey. It's fine. Gem's an apprentice. She works the desk right now because we don't have a receptionist, and the apprentice gets all the shitty jobs."

"Ah," Bailey said. "I see. So she won't feel pushed out if I take over?"

Cash chuckled, shaking his head. "No. Are you always so… painfully considerate?"

She shifted on her heels, resisting the urge to look away from his mocking smile. How could he make her feel so uncomfortable and so electrified all at once? "Do unto others," she muttered finally.

"You a Christian?" The doodle on his page was turning into a full-on work of art; a cascade of feathers, falling from a twisted, dying tree.

"No," she said. "But I used to read the Bible a lot. When I was a kid."

He raised his brows, and she raised hers. Let him question her; it was true. The Bible was the only book to be found in most hotel rooms.

And she'd spent a lot of time in hotel rooms back then.

But he let the statement pass. "What do you study?" he asked, suddenly dropping his pen again. It was as though he didn't want to hold it, but his fingers kept picking it up anyway.

"Psychology with cognitive neuroscience," she told him, her feet bringing her closer to the desk without permission. Closer to him. He watched her advance with cool certainty, as though he knew exactly how hypnotic his attention was. In the absence of another chair, she leaned against the side of his desk, and his gaze sank lazily to the place where her hip met the wood. He took his time looking, unashamed, and the bold perusal aroused her awareness. Desire, warm and languid, unfurled in Bailey's belly and took a look around. Decided it liked the view. Settled in for a while, ready to make her thighs clench and her life hell.

This man might be more than she could handle.

Cash met her eyes again, and she found herself studying the colour: cold jade shot through with flecks of molten gold. Impossible eyes.

"Are you going to psychoanalyse me?" he asked, his voice low.

"I'm not a doctor. I don't even graduate 'til July."

"But could you?"

"I don't think I'd want to," she whispered.

And just like that, the crackling energy between them was wiped out. His face was smooth as he leaned back in his chair, putting distance between them.

"Good," he said. And then, his voice strained, he continued, "When you mentioned university I thought you might be... younger than I'd hoped."

Hoped? Why would he *hope* for anything to do with her? It couldn't be the job; Gem was young, too. No; something told her Cash had slipped up with that comment, and he knew it. First he called her pretty, and now he... hoped.

"I took some time off after college," she explained. "Illness in the family."

"Oh?"

"My mother." Why was she saying this? She never said this. She usually stared in silence until the subject was changed. "Lung cancer. She died." Alone. Alone except for Bailey. Because all those men she'd spent her life chasing…

Well.

Cash cleared his throat and broke eye contact for what felt like the first time in forever. Then he was back, his gaze hypnotising her once more. Only, now, she remembered why she couldn't let him or anyone else hypnotise her. Ever. "I'm very sorry," he said, and she almost believed him. When he looked at her like this, she could pretend he was the man she'd dreamed up, rather than the man he was turning out to be.

"Also," she said, desperate to wipe the softness from his expression, "I was held back at school."

"Held back, and now you're studying neuroscience?"

She shrugged. "It's a long story."

He looked like he wanted to hear it, but the sound of laughter interrupted them, floating up from downstairs, followed by a burst of music. A distraction. Thank God.

The close, intimate air of the office dispersed, leaving behind a shabby room with too many fluorescent lights. And the softness in Cash's green eyes faded away, until only the harsh lines of his face and the sharp set of his jaw remained.

"That's the rabble," he said. "Why don't you go down and let Gem set you up? I'll sort out the forms you need by the end of the day."

"Alright." Bailey paused for a moment, leashed by a reluctant fascination with this man. Now that she'd decided Hot Coffee Guy was nothing but an illusion, she perversely wanted to see some evidence to the contrary. Some glimpse of the guy who'd charmed her with his sweet smile and gentleness.

But Cash remained a stony-faced stranger, beautiful and untouchable and so fucking hot. The sight of his broad chest and defined biceps beneath his simple black T-shirt was burned into her retinas.

There was nothing sweet about him.

With a quiet sigh, Bailey turned to leave. But as she

approached the door, she noticed a small sprig of plastic holly taped to its frame, haphazard and incongruous. It reminded her of the Christmas cheer downstairs. She looked over her shoulder at Cash and found him staring at her, his eyes full of something achingly intense, yet tender. If she didn't know better, she'd think that it was longing.

But then he cleared his throat and averted his gaze, the shutters falling once more.

"Who put this up?" she asked, pointing at the mistletoe.

He coughed. "I did, actually."

"Yeah? So you like all that stuff downstairs?"

He looked pointedly at the clock on the far wall. "You should get going. Appointments will be starting soon."

"Right," she said, and hurried off. But as she made her way downstairs, a reluctant smile curved her lips.

Maybe Hot Coffee Guy was in there somewhere.

CHAPTER 5

The rabble, as it turned out, referred to the rest of the employees.

They stood together, Gem behind the desk, two men in front of it. One was younger, brown-skinned, and handsome. The other was older, rougher, tougher; a white guy with a thick beard and heavy frown lines. All three of them were talking and laughing together, clearly close. But that stopped when Bailey came into the room.

"Hel-*lo*," the younger of the men said, straightening up immediately. He glanced at Gem. "Who's this, then?"

"That's the new girl," Gem said. She blew a bubble, let it pop, and the older man stared at her pursed lips as though they held the secret to life itself. But Gem didn't appear to notice. "She's gonna be our receptionist. So I'm finally free of the desk!"

The young man's brows shot up, practically disappearing into his razor-sharp hairline. But then a smooth smile took over his face, and he approached Bailey with practiced charm.

It was effective. But it wasn't Cash.

"I'm Jay," he grinned, holding out a hand for her to shake. He had big hands. He really was a good-looking guy. She should feel something when she put her palm against his.

But she didn't. She just shook his hand, and smiled politely, and said, "I'm Bailey."

"And this is Steve," Gem interjected, gesturing at the other man, who had a gruff shyness about him. He gave Bailey a nod, but every inch of his being was focused on Gem—like she was the sun and he the sunflower. Bailey wondered if Gem knew that this guy was in love with her.

Probably not.

"Hi," Bailey smiled, nodding back at Steve. She was about to make her way over to the desk when Jay stopped her, a frown creasing his brow.

"Have we met before?" he asked. "I feel like I recognise you from somewhere."

"Um..." Bailey wracked her mind, but came up blank. "No," she said. "I don't think so."

"Huh." He floated back over to the desk and she followed, brushing the moment off. If it was a line, it hadn't worked. Then again, he hadn't exactly followed through.

"Cash said something about you setting me up?" she asked Gem.

"Oh, yeah. I'll give you, like, a little induction. I'm kind of shit at this job though, so it won't be that great. Come round here."

Docile as a lamb, Bailey made her way to the other side of the desk. The men wandered towards the back of the shop, into another room that she could only catch a glimpse of from here. She heard them talking—well, Jay talking and Steve grunting—over the classic Christmas songs dancing through the air.

"You guys like Christmas, hm?"

Gem gave her a strange look. "*Everyone* likes Christmas."

"Well, maybe not everyone..."

"Everyone," Gem repeated firmly. "Even people who don't celebrate."

"Uh... Really?" Bailey asked doubtfully.

"Of course. They have more money for the Boxing Day sales." Gem snorted at her own joke, then reached beneath the neckline of her vest to scratch her collarbone. The movement shifted her clothing slightly—just enough for Bailey to see the lavender and indigo tattoo on the other woman's chest. It was delicately lined, surrounded by splashes of pigment that looked like a watercolour painting—a painting etched into her pale skin. Fascinated, Bailey stared at the tattoo. It was an intriguing shape—a merging of the symbols for male and female, along with a third symbol that she didn't recognise.

"What?" Gem demanded, her voice suddenly hard. "What are you looking at?"

Bailey looked up sharply. Caught staring again. Everyone would think she was some kind of weirdo."I'm sorry. I just saw your tattoo. The colours and the..." She waved her hand, unsure of how to describe it. "I've never seen one like that."

"Oh," Gem said, and the guarded panic in her eyes faded. "Right. Jay did it. Watercolour tatts. It's a cool technique."

"It's pretty."

"Thanks," Gem smiled. "Anyway, let me show you the books, okay? It's all very simple. We're kinda basic here."

They spent a cosy hour behind the desk, which was probably longer than necessary, but Bailey found herself warming to Gem. The girl was funny, and her excessive energy was endearing. They were so busy giggling together, Bailey almost didn't notice when Cash came downstairs just in time to greet his first client.

And she definitely didn't notice that the client was a beautiful, heavily tatted woman who clearly knew Cash very well.

And she *certainly* didn't notice the fact that Cash grinned when he saw the woman, or that he hugged her easily, as though it were a habit.

Nope.

Nope, nope, nope.

She didn't notice any of that.

THE LOW WHINE of the tattoo gun kept Cash in a state of meditation while he worked. He traced over the faint lines with a steady hand, falling into a familiar rhythm. Line, line, wipe. Line, line, wipe.

Charlene was sitting like a rock, as usual. She was more canvas than human, she held so still—which wasn't easy when someone was dragging a needle across the underside of your breasts, Cash was sure. It had been a three-hour session with no breaks, and her hyper-detailed, ocean-inspired sternum tattoo was almost done.

He made a few finishing touches, then turned off the gun. As the buzz receded, so did his calm. Reality came filtering in.

Fuck.

That was Bailey laughing in the next room. He'd heard her uncontrolled giggles often enough to recognise them with ease. But who the hell was making her laugh like that? His calm shattered, Cash cleaned the finished tattoo with practiced movements before covering it in clingfilm.

"You like it?" he asked Charlene. But for once, he honestly didn't care about the answer.

"Oh my God, yes," she gushed, hopping out of the chair. She stood in front of the huge mirror on the wall, twisting her slim body this way and that. She was topless—had to be, for this—and one slender arm was pressed against her full breasts, hiding her nipples from view. He knew for a fact that those nipples were cherry-red and thick, but the memory did little for him today.

Usually, Charlene was one of the women who made him regret his policy—ninety days, no going back. That was all he could offer a girl, no matter how beautiful or smart or charming she might be.

But right now, with the echo of Bailey's laughter teasing his memory, Cash didn't regret a damn thing about leaving Charlene.

Speaking of; the woman's glittering eyes met his in the

mirror. Blue. Perfectly pretty. But somehow not what he wanted to see. "You have magic hands, Cash," she murmured.

"Thanks," he said shortly.

She turned to face him, her smile wry. "I'll never convince you to break those rules of yours, will I?"

"I told you I wouldn't change my mind," he said, but this was familiar ground, so he felt comfortable enough to crack a smile.

"I didn't believe you. I should have." She sounded rueful. But then she let her gaze flit mischievously down to his crotch. "Worth it."

Cash chuckled as he left the workstation, pulling the thin curtain around it to give her some semblance of privacy. "Get dressed, Char. I'll see you out front."

He found Bailey seated behind the welcome desk, with Gem at her side. The two women appeared to be discussing some TV show about werewolves, while Jay leaned against the counter like some kind of sleaze. His white teeth were bright against his golden skin as he displayed his infamous smile. That smile had won him mountains of pussy; it was handsome, debonair despite his relative youth, and the very definition of charming.

And he was using it on Bailey.

"I *swear* I recognise you from somewhere," he was saying, his gaze a little too focused on Bailey's full lips.

Not that Cash could blame him. But he clenched his fists regardless.

"I really don't think we've met," Bailey said. "I'm good with faces."

"So am I. Comes with being an artist." Jay leaned further against the counter, making sure that his biceps flexed—and Bailey actually *smiled*, a sweet, shy smile that fired Cash's blood in more ways than one. Shit, was she falling for this line?

But then it hit him—it might not be a line. Jay might actually recognise Bailey. Because, like an idiot, Cash had been sketching out her face since the day he'd first seen her at that fucking coffee shop.

Crap.

Surging forward, Cash interrupted the happy little trio just in time to hear Jay purr, "You should come to lunch with me."

"She can't," Cash said, surprising himself. Six eyes swivelled to focus on him, all questioning. He didn't have an explanation for his vehemence. Well; not one he could say aloud.

"What do you mean?" Gem asked, her lips curling into a mischievous smile. Little trouble-maker.

Cash clenched his jaw. "I mean, Bailey can't go out for lunch. We have things to do."

"Oh, come on," Jay rolled his eyes. "Like what? You gonna show her that shitty coffee shop you like?"

Bailey's eyes slid down into her lap. She bit her lip. God, what a fucking mouth. The things Cash could do with that mouth...

"I don't know why you even go there," Gem said, and something in her voice made him suddenly nervous. "You hate fancy coffee."

That had Bailey looking up. Oh, yeah. Frowning, she asked, "You do?"

"Ah..."

"Yep," Gem confirmed gleefully. "He only drinks it black. Why he has to go to some artisanal place for a cup of black coffee is beyond me—"

"Black?" Bailey echoed. "Seriously? You only drink black coffee?"

Jay blinked, looking from Cash to Bailey with a frown. And then, all of a sudden, he remembered. Cash *saw* it. He saw the precise moment that Jay placed the woman before them. The precise moment that he realised Bailey was the girl littered throughout Cash's sketchbooks.

The younger man straightened, taking a subtle step back from the desk. "No worries," he said casually. "First-day admin. I get it. You want me to pick anything up, boss?"

Cash caught his friend's eyes, and relief flooded him as he saw understanding in their depths. "No," he said gruffly. "I'm good."

"Alright. I'll be off, then. Gem; the usual?"

"Cheers love" Gem smiled sunnily. "You're a star."

As Jay left the shop, Charlene came sauntering out from the studio, her coat slung over her shoulder and her smile wide. She was clearly giddy about her new ink. Excitement suited her. She was lovely. And he didn't give a fuck.

"Thanks for sorting me out, Cash," she murmured.

"No problem," he replied. But the weight of her questioning gaze wouldn't leave him alone. He pushed his hair out of his face, his fingers twitching with the nervous urge to pick up a pen—to put a whole world of creativity between himself and human contact.

No dice.

So, his mind racing, he reached instinctively for the closest thing to freedom.

"Bailey," he said, already turning towards the stairs. "Step into my office, will you?"

"Alright." Her voice was low, subdued. He didn't like that. But then, it was really none of his concern, was it?

"Cash," Charlene called after him. "You're going? I thought we could have lunch."

"Sorry." He mounted the first step. "Duty calls."

And then he hurried up the staircase before she could say anything else. Because while Charlene was pretty—gorgeous, really, with her red hair and doll-like features—and sweet, and fun, she was also the past. He didn't return to old conquests; not ever. She knew that.

See, keeping someone around for too long meant becoming attached, and Cash didn't do attached.

He simply couldn't. Attachment was dangerous.

For the second time in one day, Bailey found herself watching Cash from across a desk.

The situation wasn't quite as uncomfortable this time, though. Now that she'd found her confidence, she'd dragged another chair up rather than standing like a child waiting to be scolded.

His auburn hair fell forward, hiding his face in shadow as he bent over the documents in front of him. Then he looked up, and her heart almost stopped at the sudden sight of those sharp, green eyes. *Damn. Warn a girl, would you?*

"Here you go," he said gruffly, pushing the papers towards her. "You got a P45?"

"No. And I'm not going back there to get one, either." She bit her lip. "Michael's like a gremlin. A very angry gremlin with a shiny head. I don't think I can face him."

He chuckled as he handed her a pen—though she noticed that he didn't let his skin touch hers. "I wouldn't expect you to," he said. "They'll probably post it, anyway."

"Maybe." She began filling out the form, the act familiar to her. She'd spent her life following her mother, who'd spent hers following men. Starting a new job was nothing new.

Of course, her new boss was the definition of uncharted territory. But the job itself? At least she could handle that.

"So," she said as she signed and dated the form. "Black coffee, hm?" She looked up to find him... blushing?

Holy shit. Her big, tatted biker boss was blushing. It was an adorably faint flush that tinged his high cheekbones. Perils of being a red-head, she supposed. Add it to the list of things about him that made absolutely no sense—right next to his apparent love of Christmas decorations.

"About that," he began.

"Yeah?" She raised her brows, trying not to smile.

"I was just trying to broaden my horizons."

"Ah. Hence the *Surprise me*?"

"Yep."

He looked stiff as a board. His fingers flexed, and somehow she knew that he was searching for a pen. But *she* had his pen. Let him try to hide without it. Perhaps it was the sound of *All I Want*

For Christmas Is You floating up from downstairs, but Bailey felt mischievous. She leaned forward, a teasing smile on her face, and asked, "Did you finish *any* of the coffee I made you?"

"Ah..."

"Oh my Lord." She gasped, her smile widening. "You didn't, did you?"

He muttered something she couldn't quite hear.

"What?"

"I said I—" with a sigh, he broke off, raking a hand through his hair. She caught a glimpse of the dark ink swirling up to his knuckles, identifying the image for the first time; a cloudy night, the stylised moon hanging amidst stars and darkness.

"Go on," she prompted, barely hiding her smirk. There was something about seeing a bad boy blush that made her desperate to keep the moment going.

His eyes flashed as he finally blurted out his answer. "I like watching you make all those drinks. It's like a little dance you do, and you look so happy, and you love mixing shit up..."

Bailey paused, his response unexpected. He waited, clearly uncomfortable, while the implications of his statement filtered through her mind.

"Wow," she said slowly. "You're a sweetheart, aren't you?"

He crossed his arms. "What the hell does that mean?"

"It means that I have no idea why you act like such an arse sometimes, but it's not real. You're actually a nice guy."

"Nice guys finish last," he muttered. But he was blushing again. And something about the set of his lips beneath all that stubble made her think that he was secretly pleased.

"Boring guys finish last," she corrected, pushing the completed forms back to him. "Nice guys finish anywhere they want. Especially when they look like you."

And then, before she could say anything else wildly inappropriate, she got up and left the room.

But she let her hips sway, just a little, as she went—because

God damn it, Hot Coffee Guy was the real deal. And she was absolutely sure that he'd be looking.

CHAPTER 6

Nice guys finish anywhere they want.

That phrase rung through Cash's mind like a church bell as he sat in the office, frantically sketching on the back of... an order form for fresh needles? Whatever. His sketchbook was somewhere around the shop—probably at his workstation—but inspiration had him by the balls. If he got up to look for the right materials, he'd lose the magic.

His hands worked frantically, marking out the concept with harsh, black lines. Once upon a time, an art teacher had told him he should only ever sketch in pencil. But biro was Cash's medium of choice; let the mistakes sit there for everyone to see. He'd recreate again and again until it was just right, and then he'd put it into someone's skin and every flaw would have been worth it.

But whose body would this latest fantasy adorn? He had no idea.

What the hell had she meant, *finish anywhere they want?* Surely not the filthy interpretation that his mind immediately latched on to. She was too sweet for that.

But then, she'd called *him* sweet, hadn't she? And here he was, dreaming of the pretty patterns his come would paint against her dark skin. Ah, fuck. He still couldn't decide who and what she was—dream or reality? White silk or red latex?

Maybe she was both.

Didn't matter. He'd never fucking know. Because if he let himself get close to a girl like that, he wouldn't be able to stick to his own rules. Adoration would set in, obsession would follow—and then he would finally become his father. Whether he liked it or not. Whether he wanted it or not. He—

No.

Cash's hand moved frantically, scarring the paper. He pressed harder, worked faster, as though he could carve away the twisted voices in his head. He knew what they were, of course. Intrusive thoughts, his therapist had called them. They didn't come from him; they came from his monster. He also knew that he was supposed to ignore them, but it was pretty fucking hard to ignore something that went on inside your own mind.

Still; he'd try his best. That was all he could ever do.

"What you working on there, mate?"

Cash looked up to find Steve entering the office, his own sketchbook tucked under his brawny arm.

"Uh..." The order form now bore the image of a woman, her long hair swirling about her shoulders like living wind, pointed little horns atop her head. The woman's face was wickedly gleeful as she brought her fingers up to her mouth, her dark eyes flashing behind her glasses. Tiny fangs peeked out from full lips, and her tongue was in the act of sliding out to taste the droplets on her fingertips.

Fuck. He'd drawn Bailey.

Again.

"Nothing," he lied.

"Really?" Steve ambled over to his own desk, his slow movement and gentle tone deceptive as always, hiding the sharp intellect beneath. When he spoke again, his voice was quiet. "Because it looks a hell of a lot like Bailey."

Cursing, Cash flipped over the page. He was acting like a

fucking teenager, and he knew it. But he wasn't about to back down in his own shop.

"It's nothing," he repeated tersely.

Steve gave him a level look. "You know, in my time I've learned that you should grab a good thing with both hands. Before it disappears."

Cash arched a brow. "Yeah? So when were you planning on *grabbing* Gem?"

The temperature of the office dropped until it almost matched the icy street below. Steve's mouth twisted into a grim line and he folded his arms, leaning back in his seat.

"You know I can't do a thing for Gem," he said, his voice a brick wall.

"What I *know* is that you're as much of a coward as I am. So you can hold the inspiring speech."

For a moment, the men stared each other down, the atmosphere tense. But then Steve let out a grudging chuckle, shaking his head. "Right pair of twats we both are," he said gruffly.

Relieved, Cash rolled his eyes. "You're not wrong."

"You done for the day?"

"Nah. My next client's in at—" Cash glanced at the clock on the wall. "Oh, shit."

Steve smirked. "Lose track of time?"

Snorting, Cash ignored the other man's words. Somehow, his lunch hour had dwindled away to nothing, and now he had less than ten minutes to call John. Cursing himself, he pulled up the hotel's website and dialled their number, keeping one eye on the clock.

"Hi," he said, after an exceptionally cheerful man greeted him. "Could I speak to, ah...John, please? Room 302?"

"Mr Halliday? Certainly, Sir. I'll put you through now."

"Thank you."

There were a few, long beeps. A few too many, maybe. Cash started to wonder where John was. Started to hope the young man hadn't done anything stupid, the way Cash might've done once.

But then the beeps disappeared, and a familiar voice said, "Hello?"

"John," he replied, relieved. "It's Cash."

"Oh, hi!"

"I'm really sorry, but I have to make this quick. I've got a client coming in soon. I just wanted to let you know that I spoke to my friend about you last night, and he wants to meet you to discuss a job."

"What? Are you serious?"

"Dead serious. He's the director of a non-profit for disadvantaged groups in the area. He wants to talk to you about an administrative role and maybe some kind of mentoring position."

John was quiet for a moment. When he finally spoke, his voice was suspiciously hoarse. "Thank you. This is fucking unbelievable. I—I can't believe this is happening."

"You don't need to thank me. I..." Cash looked over at Steve, who was bent busily over his own desk, pencil in hand. "Let's just say I've been where you are right now. But listen, I need to go. And we need to get you a mobile, too, so you're not waiting around in the hotel room for me to call you."

"Oh, don't worry about that. Bailey rang me earlier, and she's coming over tomorrow night with a spare phone of hers."

Cash swallowed the lump that suddenly materialised in his throat. His eyes fell towards the drawing in front of him as he traced its stark lines, the slight indent his pen strokes had made in the paper. "Yeah? That's nice of her."

"She's a great girl. And she mentioned that you gave her a job?"

"Yeah, well. We needed a receptionist at my studio."

"Did you? Because the way she was talking, it seems the job's pretty light." John's tone became playful. "She didn't say anything, but it made me wonder if you had some other motivation for hiring her?"

"What? No." Cash ran his hands through his hair, pushing the strands back irritably. He should get it cut soon. It was fucking annoying.

"You sure? Because women aren't really my cup of tea, but even I can see Bailey's appeal."

Yeah. Cash bet he could. Bailey's *appeal* was probably visible from halfway across the planet.

"Listen, John, I've got to go. I'll be in touch. You've got my number?"

"Yep," the other man said, his voice rich with amusement.

"Alright. Uh… Talk soon."

"Bye. And thanks again, Cash. Seriously."

"Stop thanking me." He put the phone down.

Then he wasted a few precious minutes staring down at the picture he'd drawn of Bailey. Tracing the contours of her face with a practiced eye. He'd got the nose slightly off—it was broader, flatter on the bridge. Her brows were higher, more finely arched. But he'd got the plump cheeks just right, along with the soft lips that could go from sweet to sensual in five minutes flat. And most importantly, he thought, he'd captured that gleam in her eyes; the one that spoke of whole-hearted enthusiasm, of the adorable way she threw herself into everything and thoroughly enjoyed it, even if she became embarrassed a moment later. He knew her face well. He'd drawn her often.

Too fucking often.

Attachment was a dangerous thing.

Cash tore the picture in two.

CHAPTER 7

"What are you doing tonight?" Gem asked, throwing a lilac rucksack over one shoulder. It was covered in bright, bold pins; from torn-up teddy bears to declarations of a femme revolution. And there was a little Slytherin badge on the corner, too.

Bailey smiled at the sight as she packed up her own boring bag and threw on her coat. "Going to the library, I think. I need to get started on my January assignments."

"Ugh. Kill me now." Gem rolled her eyes as she switched off the Christmas tree's lights for the night. "You couldn't pay me to go back to school."

"Sadly, I'm paying them."

"More fool you, chick." She threw a cheeky smile over her shoulder as she headed for the door, strutting away in her pink Doc Martens. "Look, it's the weekend. If you change your mind, I'm meeting some mates for a drink tonight. Text me, yeah?"

"Maybe," Bailey smiled. She wasn't exactly in the habit of going out; saving money was a serious business. Or maybe the few years spent waiting in the backroom of a nightclub while her mother bartended had put her off the idea for life.

Whatever. She tried not to examine those kinds of thoughts too closely.

The music was gone and the Christmas lights were dark. Still, the tinsel pinned to the front desk rustled at her cheerfully as she brushed past it, heading towards the studio. The lights in there had been left on. She'd just sort them out, she thought, before leaving for the day…

The studio at Fallen Tattoos was as professional and sterile as the front of the shop was quirky. Jay had explained that Cash took trust seriously: the customers needed to know that their bodies weren't about to be defaced, or worse, actually harmed. And so, the studio maintained an almost hospital-like aura, ensuring customers felt utterly safe there. It was an interesting approach, one that made her wonder what Cash had seen and experienced while touring the world. And maybe if he'd ever had a negative experience of his own when it came to his countless tattoos. She'd like to ask him about the ink covering his body—or at least, what she'd seen of it.

And maybe now was her chance. Because here he was, sitting at his workstation, leaning over one of the huge, electric chairs that clients lay or sat on while being inked. His hand worked busily, darting back and forth over a page in his sketchbook, the strokes bold and aggressive. She'd assumed that he was upstairs, in the office.

"Hey," she said. He didn't seem to hear her, hadn't even noticed her come in. And she'd certainly had no inkling that he was there; he was utterly silent, focused, as though his art took him far away from this little shop tucked into the grey city streets.

"Cash," she said, louder this time. The sound jolted him out of his trance, and he looked up at her with unfocused eyes. The usually harsh lines of his face were soft, the way they might be in sleep, and there was no cruel curl to his mouth.

She might have imagined seeing him this way—utterly relaxed, unaware—once or twice. Or ten times. Hey; most guys fell asleep after sex, right? And Bailey strove for accuracy in all of her masturbation fantasies.

A girl had to have creative standards.

"Bailey," he murmured, his eyes finally focusing on her.

She smiled.

And then, of course, he ruined it.

"What are you doing here?" he demanded, his gaze hardening. He glared at her as though she'd been spying, and shut his sketchbook closed with a snap. "You should've left already."

"Um… I was just checking that all the lights were off before I went."

"Why? I can do that. Before I lock up."

She raised her eyebrows. "Well, excuse me for helping. I won't bother again."

"Bailey," he sighed, "there's no need to be dramatic."

Dramatic? Bailey's temper rarely came out to play, but when it did, it tended to run away with her.

She employed her most precise diction as she replied, taking care to make each consonant as sharp as could be—she didn't want him to miss a single syllable. Her smile sweet and her words slow, Bailey said simply: "Go fuck yourself, Cash Evans."

As she turned on her heel, she saw his jaw drop from the corner of her eye. But he didn't say a single thing in response as she stormed off.

Fucking *men*. Bailey slammed the shop door behind her before trudging through the icy night. Her breath plumed in front of her face as she muttered to herself, jamming her frozen hands into her pockets. There wasn't a man on earth who didn't develop an attitude when he thought he could get away with it—she was convinced. Give them a taste of sweetness and watch them come over all high and mighty.

Her knowledge was hard-won, gained through watching her mother make a fool of herself for men who turned crueler the softer she became. There was one sure-fire way to turn a prince into a frog: show him a little kindness. She should never have allowed herself to like Cash, even a little bit.

When someone viewed you as an object, every interaction became transactional—and the sad truth was that to many men, a woman could be nothing *but* an object. Maybe a trophy, maybe a childhood blanket, maybe a piece of rubbish. It made no difference. She'd learned long ago to leash her emotions around men she might desire. At the end of the day, most of them were only good for one thing.

She chanted under her breath, in time with the stamp of her feet against the pavement. "Remember that. Remember that. Remember that."

CHAPTER 8

On Sunday evening, Bailey knocked at John's bland hotel door. When it swung open, she held up her shopping bags, a wide smile on her face. "Knock knock, bitch!"

"Ugh, it's you." John rolled his eyes. "I was hoping for the hot tattoo artist." But then he broke into a smile of his own, and she knew he was glad to see her.

"Shut up," she smirked as she pushed past him into the hotel room, dropping her bags on the table. "I come bearing gifts!"

"Like I haven't had a lifetime's worth of Christmas blessings in the past few days."

She gave him a look before taking off her coat. "Look, here's the phone. I got you a SIM too—"

"Oh, Bailey."

"And some gingerbread." He sat down next to her on the carpet as she emptied out her bags. "And a couple of Chocolate Oranges. They're buy-one-get-one-free at Tesco's. And some little mince pies, look, and a Christmas nibbles selection."

"Bailey." He raised his brows as he surveyed the junk food. "This isn't all for me, is it?"

"Well..."

"Let me guess: you'd be happy to help?"

She laughed guiltily. "Only if you'll have me."

"Of course I'll have you! In fact, there's lots we need to discuss..."

John clambered onto the bed and arranged their feast while Bailey popped the room's little kettle on.

"The phone is just in time," he grinned. "I have a *very* important number to put in it."

"Oh?" She added two sugars to John's tea and one to her own, thinking happily about how much fuller his cheeks looked already, and the way his eyes sparkled.

"Yep. My *potential* new boss."

"What?!" She came over to the bed, clutching the cups of tea.

"Cash has sorted me an interview already!"

"Seriously?"

"*And* he's taking me out to get a suit tomorrow."

Bailey handed John his cup before taking a sip of her own. She wasn't sure what to make of this new information. Yes, she'd known that Cash was... kind. But since the disaster of yesterday evening, she'd maintained the sort of frosty energy towards him that made it easy to forget he was capable of things like this.

"You're awfully quiet," John murmured, breaking open the plastic tub of gingerbread. "I thought he might have mentioned it to you."

"Hm?"

"You know." He eyed her closely. "At work?"

"Oh. Um... We don't really talk much. I'm just the receptionist, and he's some kind of tattoo god."

"What does *that* mean?"

"You know I saw him in a magazine? Apparently, he spent years touring the world and tattooing celebrities and whatever."

"Really?" John considered that for a moment. "Makes sense. I knew he was loaded."

"Loaded?"

"My instincts never lie. Which is also how I know that something's going on between you two."

Bailey stared, flabbergasted. When a bite of mince pie threatened to fall out of her mouth, she finally clamped her jaw shut. "Oh, my God," she frowned. "No. Nope. Sorry, man. The instincts are way off, there."

"What's that old quote about protesting too much?"

"Shut up."

"You're telling me you don't want to smash him to smithereens?"

Bailey almost choked on her own spit. "Shut *up!*"

"All I'm saying is, you could do worse." John lowered his gaze demurely, fiddling with his sleeves. Sometime in the last two days, he'd bought a pair of striped pyjamas. He looked unfairly adorable, considering he was such a demon.

"I could *not* do worse than Cash Evans. Trust me on that."

"Hmmm," John mumbled around a mouthful of gingerbread, spraying crumbs across his sheets. "I smell drama."

"Don't speak with your mouth full."

"Drama waits for no man, or manners."

Bailey rolled her eyes. "I'll admit, I thought he was cute, back when he used to come into the coffee shop. But you already knew that. Now I'm getting to know him better, he's… hot and cold. I don't like it. That shit's manipulative."

John chewed thoughtfully before he answered. "Ordinarily I'd agree with you," he said. "But I swear down, he might be the sweetest man I've ever met. He's very 'tortured artist'. You know?"

"'Tortured artist' is code for 'attractive arsehole'."

"Only when they're faking it. Have you considered that he might have some genuine baggage?"

Bailey shrugged. Truthfully, no; she hadn't considered that at all. But it opened up a whole new world of potential problems.

"I'm just saying. Everyone has baggage. Don't you?"

"Well, yeah." She admitted reluctantly.

"But you're still an amazing person. I think any man would be lucky to have you."

"Aw, John." She slapped his skinny shoulder playfully. "Stop."

"*And* I'm sure you want to think that someone, somewhere, might be willing to help you through that baggage instead of letting it push them away."

The teasing smile slid off Bailey's face as she considered that statement. She didn't want that—did she?

No. She didn't want any man. Or at least, not in *that* way. Semi-regular hookups did her just fine, thank you very much. And for the all-too-often times that she couldn't bear to go out on the hunt—to glam herself up and keep her mouth shut long enough to seduce a man—well. It was the 21st Century. Thank you, baby Jesus, for the blessing of vibrators.

Sure; every now and then, she might indulge in the odd romance novel. And she swooned over the growing intimacy, the heartfelt declarations, the intense adoration, just like anyone else. But that was a fantasy. It didn't mean anything. Or at least, she *might* be able to convince herself of that, if it weren't for the fact that she studied psychology. But Bailey knew better. Fantasies always meant something. The question was, what?

"I suppose you might be right," she murmured.

"I usually am."

"Hm." She put down the rest of her mince pie, her thoughts splitting into a thousand overwhelming pieces.

"Just think about it, why don't you?"

As though she could do anything else.

CHAPTER 9

John's words continued to haunt her, but so did her own.

Go fuck yourself, Cash Evans.

She heard them every time she saw Cash around the shop, every time he asked her stiffly about appointments and whenever she passed him the phone. They danced around each other like strangers for almost a week, and she spent her time off wondering how she'd ever come back from the gauntlet she'd thrown down.

Not that he'd retaliated at all. Infuriating fucker.

He just looked at her in that way of his, with those gleaming predator's eyes. She developed a worrying obsession with cataloging his ink. He only ever wore T-shirts, so all she'd seen so far was the full sleeve on his right arm—which disappeared up under his clothing and spread down to his knuckles—and the piece on his left forearm. The former was an inverted landscape, from the cloudy night sky on his hand and wrist, rising up to black, jagged trees—bare of leaves—and then further into the earth, where gems and fossils hid. The latter was an underwater scene, featuring an octopus that wound its way over his skin, elbow to wrist. She studied the artwork covertly, drinking in snatches every time he passed by the front desk, lowering her gaze when he looked over at her.

And when he was working, she rifled through the magazine she'd found on her first day at Fallen, reading the feature on him.

He'd denied an interview—as was his habit, apparently. It was his social media presence, his direct and unassuming contact with clients and fans, that had propelled him into the spotlight. His distinctive style and undeniable skills had kept him there. His gorgeous face and bad boy charm had made him all his money.

And he had a lot of money. The article took pains to make that clear. It mentioned something else, too: his mysterious, dark past, the details of which were largely unknown. The fact that his privacy was widely considered to hide an internal conflict that his art only hinted at. And his love for his family, his mother and sister. Apparently, the first major purchase he'd made with his newfound riches was a big old house for his mother in some quiet, country village.

This knowledge highlighted the issue that was really getting under her skin: who the hell was Cash Evans? Because, for all her pseudo-stalking, Bailey could honestly say that she had no idea.

A week after her night in with John, Bailey was just slipping in her earphones and opening her music app when his name flashed up on her caller ID. She grinned. His irreverence was just what she needed right now.

"Night, guys," Gem called as she and Steve left, heading for the pub, no doubt.

"Night." Bailey waved back absently. Then, accepting the call, she demanded, "Spill! Tell me all! Immediately!"

"Give me a second woman, bloody hell!" John laughed down the phone, his broad, Northern vowels filling her ears. "You still at work?"

"Are *you* still at work?" John had aced his interview, and today had been his very first day at his brand new job as an administrative assistant.

"I just left," he said smugly. "Working life, you know."

"Oh, yes, darling," Bailey drawled jokingly. "Quite."

"Is Cash around?"

At the mention of Cash's name, Bailey felt her smile slip. "Um… I think so? Last I saw him, he was heading up to the office."

"Great. Go and get him! I need to tell both of you about this at once."

Bailey faltered, her mind working frantically to come up with some excuse. But she couldn't let whatever petty issues lay between her and Cash ruin John's big moment. With a resigned sigh, she slid off her chair and walked out from behind the welcome desk.

"Alright," she relented. "Give me a sec."

"Hurry up! I have so much to tell you, honestly."

"I bet, Mr… Mr. Professional Man."

"Ah, Bailey. That razor-sharp wit never gets old."

"Shut up." She jogged up the stairs and along the corridor, her nerves mounting at the sight of the closed office door. Taking a deep breath, she stepped towards the foreboding entrance…

Only for the door to swing open, light spilling out for a fraction of a second before it was blocked by Cash's large body. He stepped out into the hall, his movements as decisive as ever, and barrelled right into her.

Bailey cried out as she stumbled back. Though she'd long since swapped sensible heels and skirt-suits for jeans and Converse, matching the casual style of her colleagues, her feet appeared determined to embarrass her.

But just before she truly fell onto her arse, Cash's big hands shot out to grab her. And, of course, he managed to get a firm handful of the biggest damn part of her. His fingers sank into her hips as he dragged her up against him, bringing her into the safe zone of his body. Her hands rose automatically to press against his chest, broad and firm and hot beneath her palms.

She took a moment to catch her breath, her head spinning. Hesitantly, she looked up and found his mesmerising eyes on her.

His lips parted as he stared at her like she was the biggest surprise of his life.

"Bailey," he said softly, his hands tightening around her.

"Cash," she breathed.

"What the hell's going on?!" John squawked in her ear.

Fuck.

Sharply, she stepped away from the tempting heat of Cash's body, planting her feet firmly on the ground this time. Slapping a plastic smile onto her face, she pulled her phone out of her pocket and held it up to him, shaking it awkwardly as if to say *Ta-dah!*

"Guess who I have on the phone?" she asked, her voice artificially light.

Cash cleared his throat, the vulnerability in his expression disappearing like sunlight behind the clouds. He folded his arms and leaned against the doorway, his usual smirk firmly in place. "Let me think. John?"

"How did you know?"

"I can hear the screeching from here."

"Are you talking about me?" John demanded. "Put me on speaker!"

Bailey rolled her eyes. "Wait a minute, will you?" And then, to Cash: "He wants to tell us both about his day at the same time."

"Very egalitarian," Cash murmured. He turned and led her into the office, where Jay was working over at his desk in the corner. The younger man gave her a distracted nod before focusing on his laptop screen once more.

"Keep the earphones in," Cash said as he sat down. She perched on the edge of his desk, a quizzical frown on her face. Then he reached up and tugged one earphone from her ear. Quickly, she understood.

Her heart suddenly thumping, she shuffled around until she was sat facing him, she on the desk, he in his chair. She leaned forward, face in her hands, elbows against her knees, until they were close enough to share. She could feel the heat of his breath against her cheek, but she kept her eyes down, which was a mistake. Had his thighs always looked so fucking good in a pair of jeans? …And was that his—?

Nope. Nope, nope, nope. Bailey reigned in her rampant thoughts, dragged her eyes away, and focused on the conversation at hand.

"Alright," she said. "Cash is listening."

"Hey John," Cash chimed in. "How was it?"

"Oh, you'll wish you never asked!" John launched into an excited play-by-play of his first day on the job, his enthusiasm contagious. As he gushed about his experiences, Bailey found herself sharing more than just space and a phone with Cash. They laughed together, exchanging amused looks and happy smiles. By the time the call ended, she felt as though the ghost of her temper was finally laid to rest. The trap of her own anger disappeared, and so did her resentment towards Cash's on-off attitude. She remembered what John had told her about baggage.

It was possible that her own issues played a role in this too. Because when it came down to it, she wanted Cash. Badly. And if she was honest with herself, she hated that.

Still chuckling at John's bubbling wit—his impressions of the people he'd met that day had been hysterical—Bailey slid her phone back into her pocket and clambered off of Cash's desk. She knew by now that she wasn't imagining things when his gaze darted momentarily down to her arse.

He wanted her. And maybe he hated that, too.

"You guys are doing a great thing, you know."

Bailey's head whipped around at the sound of Jay's voice, her own hair smacking her in the face. Jay'd been so quiet, she'd forgotten he was there.

"What do you mean?" she asked.

He gave her a look. "With that guy you're helping. The homeless guy."

Bailey shrugged, uncomfortable. "He's my friend. Anyway, I'm not doing anything. It's Cash."

But Cash hooked his thick arms behind his head, tossing his hair out of his face. She couldn't escape his piercing gaze as he argued, "I've got money to burn. You're paying for his phone."

"It was an old phone. I just put credit on his SIM."

He arched a brow.

"Everyone needs a phone," she insisted, fiddling with her hair self-consciously. "You can't keep a job without a phone."

"Whatever," Jay interjected, closing his laptop and standing up. "All I'm saying is, most people wouldn't make friends with a homeless person. They'd just write him off as some drug addicted loser and say he should pull himself up by his bootstraps." He paused on his way out of the room. "And I know that Cash always does this sort of thing. Share the wealth. But you, Bailey? I don't know. Most people wouldn't take the time." He shrugged. "Anyway, I better go. I have *Bake Off* reruns to watch."

"See you," Cash called.

Bailey said nothing. She was too busy thinking about what Jay had just inadvertently revealed.

Cash always does this sort of thing.

It was just a small piece of the puzzle that was Cash, but a certain picture was beginning to take shape.

They sat in silence. Cash leaned comfortably back in his chair, watching Bailey in that shameless way that usually made her want to blush—but she refused to give in to that impulse now. Instead, she faced him head-on, making her own leisurely perusal, revelling in her newfound freedom. All this time, she'd been catching the odd ray of his beauty, when all she really needed to do was grow a pair and bask in direct sunlight. He raked his gaze unapologetically over her chest—not that there was much to see—her hips, and her thighs. Then her lips; always, he went back to her lips. She conducted her own bold study, her focus shifting indecisively from his hands—so big and yet so dextrous, fingers stained with ink—to his broad shoulders, to the hair she longed to run her own fingers through. The air stirred, shimmered.

Then the door slammed downstairs, sending ripples through the molten heat that grew between them.

"Were you ever homeless?" she asked. The words ran into one another like train carriages, and she fought the urge to wring her hands, to take the question back and return to polite distance.

There was a moment when she thought he might tell her to piss off. But then he heaved out a sigh. "Yep. For a little while, as a kid."

"I see."

"My mother, my sister and I. It's not quite how people envision it to be, or it wasn't for us—maybe because we were a family. My mother was terrified that social services might take us away, so she got creative. It was less homelessness, more an abundance of other people's homes. Long rides on the night bus to places we had no business being, and then another long ride back, just so no-one could report a woman sleeping with her kids on a park bench."

Cash didn't stop talking so much as he ran out of words. He looked shocked at his own verbosity, and he wasn't the only one; she didn't think she'd ever heard him talk so much.

He drummed his fingers against the desk, reached for a pen, and grabbed the nearest scrap of paper. She knew what he'd do next, or she thought she did.

But he didn't do it. He didn't draw himself into a whole new world. He dropped the pen, looked up at her with fire in his eyes, and spoke. "Why were you held back?"

"What?" She frowned, confused by the sudden change in topic.

"You told me once that you were held back in school. I want to know why."

Ah. *I showed you mine, now show me yours.*

Well. Maybe she owed him that. But she wasn't sure how to begin.

"We moved around a lot. My mother had a problem, I suppose. With men. Not even men—she was addicted to romance. She wanted to be adored. But adoration doesn't last. It's like champagne; you have to drink it to enjoy it. Keep hold of it for too long, just to watch the bubbles dance, and it'll go flat." She sighed, already feeling disloyal. But something about setting these words free felt cathartic.

After a moment, she forged on. "See, my mother was very beautiful. Everyone told her so. She had, you know... curly hair, coloured eyes. She used to watch Disney princess films. We'd watch them together. Her favourite was *Cinderella*."

"What was your favourite?" he asked, startling her.

But she smiled when the question sunk in. "*Beauty and the Beast*. My mother said it was boring. And she didn't understand why anyone would want a beastly prince." Bailey laughed softly at the memory of her mother's theatrical scoffs. "But she liked the songs. So we'd get to watch it often enough.

"Mother—I called her Dorothy. So people wouldn't think she was old. She was very glamorous. A jet-setter. She was married four times, the first time to my father, who died. In between marriages, she ran around looking for the next prince charming, you know? When she was young, she worked as a croupier at a casino. That's how she met my dad. By the time he died, she was the one draped in diamonds at the gambling table, but that didn't last very long. Dorothy had atrocious taste in men. So we would move and move and move—because she had to live with her latest love, who happened to hail from Portsmouth or Manchester or Cambridge. Or we would move because we found ourselves *financially embarrassed*, as she used to say, and we had to disappear on our debtors." Bailey licked her lips, her mouth dry.

"So you were homeless too," Cash said.

She blinked. "No. No, we never were."

But he looked at her steadily. "Doesn't sound like you ever had a home."

She stared for a moment, her mind turning that statement over and over. Then she said, "I have to go."

And she felt his eyes on her as she fled.

CHAPTER 10

Over the course of the next few days, they reached a kind of uneasy truce. Neither mentioned the secrets they had shared. Cash continued to stare at Bailey with hunger written across his face, and she continued to pretend not to notice.

But at least now, they spoke. And sometimes he showed her a flash of the light-hearted banter, of the sweet charm, that she'd gotten to know at the coffee shop. In fact, she'd started to think of him as a cup of coffee: black, with a shot of gingerbread syrup curled up at the bottom.

Someone just needed to stir him up and make him sweet all the way through.

Almost two weeks after she began working at Fallen, he spent three hours with a regular customer of his, Gareth; an older guy who seemed to be going through some sort of midlife crisis, and definitely had the money to fund it. She often overheard Cash gently steering him away from some of his more radical tattoo ideas, presenting him with classic, neo-traditional options that suited his style way better—the diamond stud in his droopy ear notwithstanding.

Cash walked out of the studio with Gareth, shaking the other man's hand with a grin. Bailey knew that grin by now; it was the expression of pure elation that always took over his face when he'd just finished a tattoo. If she didn't know any better, she'd think he got off on torturing people.

But in reality, he was addicted to the thrill of creating. She understood because she recognised it. Oh, she wasn't a creator—she couldn't draw or write or even cook for shit. But that thrill of joy, of pure pleasure, was something she knew well. She tasted it for herself every time she sank into a fictional world—be it Harry Potter's or Merlin's or one of the Disney princesses she still geeked out over to this day.

Not that anyone needed to know about that.

She stifled a jaw-cracking yawn as Cash walked his client out. But as soon as he'd waved the man off, he was back, watching her with an intimidating frown.

"Why are you so tired?" he asked sharply.

Gem, who was making tea for herself and Jay at the machine in the corner, looked at Bailey with her brows raised. Cash didn't usually speak in quite so... *emphatic* a tone.

With a frown of her own, Bailey shrugged. "I'm not. I just—"

"Yes, you are. You've been yawning constantly for days."

"Um..." She looked over at Gem for assistance. The traitor gave her a wink before scurrying out of the room.

Drat.

Cash stalked over to the front desk, resting his forearms against its black surface. The tinsel Gem had strung along its edge was squashed as he leaned forward, studying her closely.

"You have dark circles under your eyes," he finally said.

She pursed her lips. "It's impolite to comment on a lady's appearance."

A slight blush flooded his cheeks, and she almost melted. How could someone so infuriating be so damned adorable?

But then the blush faded, replaced by a slight smile. "What if I told you that you're beautiful?"

That tore her humour in two. She felt her mouth hang open;

then she snapped it shut so fast, she was sure he must have heard her teeth click. "Don't take the piss," she gritted out.

He frowned. "I'm not. I mean what I say, and I say what I mean."

"I bet," she muttered acidly. "Listen. Beauty is like a firework: it shines. You stare. And then it's gone. Mentioning it is just as pointless."

He pulled back, his teasing air gone. Of course. Bailey wasn't like her mother and never had been. She couldn't take a compliment. She couldn't make a man feel like he was ten feet tall. She had no desire to do so. But still, she mourned the loss of his smile.

To change the subject, to smooth things over, she admitted, "My boiler's fucked."

"Beg your pardon?"

"My boiler's fucked. Heating won't work. Too cold to sleep, so I spend all night in the library at uni."

"Seriously?"

"Oh, yeah. It's exam season; it's open 24 hours right now."

"Bailey. I meant, seriously, you can't sleep in your own home?"

She shrugged, uncomfortable with the intensity of his stare. "Student landlords. Notoriously shoddy. But they'll get around to it."

He pushed his hair out of his face irritably. "Fuckers. You should have told me. I'll come over and fix it for you."

"Um. What? You can do that?"

"Of course I can. I'll nip home and get some tools at lunch, yeah?"

She blinked.

"And I'll come over after work, if that's okay?"

"Yeah. Okay. That—that would be amazing."

And that's how she ended up sitting behind Cash Evans on his terrifyingly huge motorbike, whipping through the city like something out of a U.S. blockbuster.

She had a pair of wooly gloves stuffed into her coat pocket, but she hadn't wanted to put them on. The thought of losing her grip on Cash and flying off the back of his bike was not a welcome one. Her fingers were stiff with cold as she laced them over his belly, but that wasn't enough to distract her from the wave of sensations crashing over her.

Slicing through the air at this speed felt like something close to magic, like living within the wind itself. If Cash hadn't insisted that she wear a helmet, her locs would be billowing out behind her like May Day streamers. The powerful thrum of the engine between her legs was only beaten by the irresistible pull of the body pressed against hers. Could he tell that she was drinking this experience down like hot chocolate on a winter's night? That her firm grip was less fear and more a fascination with ridges of muscle she swore she could feel right through his leather jacket?

She was playing with fire, here. She knew that. She just hadn't expected it to burn so good.

Bailey's student accommodation was a block of flats situated above a pizza place and was largely occupied by post-grads. So there were no wild parties going on as she let Cash into her pathetic little studio room, fighting embarrassment. There was no shame in her circumstances; she worked hard, she studied hard, and her flat was perfectly tidy. That's what she told herself as he stepped into the room, his eyes taking in the whole thing with one sweep.

She followed his gaze as she shut the front door. A kitchenette stood on one side of the room, the tiles on the floor transitioning to wood as it turned into a meagre living-cum-sleep space. Her bed was pushed against the far wall, by the window, with a series of pretty screens stationed around it for some modicum of privacy. The screens had belonged to her mother. They were one of the few things of hers that Bailey had kept.

Another was the little jewellery cabinet that sat on the rickety drawers in which her clothes lay. Aside from all that, the largest piece of furniture in the room was the table that separated the kitchen from everything else, on which piles of books and her crappy old laptop sat. At least the bathroom was separate, like a tiny ensuite. Still, it wasn't the greatest place she'd ever lived.

She turned to look at Cash, unsure of what she'd see in his face. But she shouldn't have worried.

"You like Christmas," he chuckled. A few steps of his booted feet took him to the cheap little Christmas tree she'd already put up and decorated. Lights hung along her window and across her bed, though they weren't turned on.

"Yeah," she said. "Doesn't everyone?"

"You'd be surprised."

She headed to the kitchenette. "Tea?"

"Please. Where's your boiler?"

Bailey showed him the little boiler hidden away in a kitchen cupboard, and he put his toolkit on the counter and got to work.

"My mother took Christmas very seriously," she said as she stirred in the milk—a little for him, a lot for her. "It was the one time of year I knew I'd have her undivided attention."

"What about your birthday?"

She smiled. "That day was her celebration, actually. Since she gave birth, and all."

"Really?" He stuck his head out from the cupboard. "Never heard anything like that."

"I took it as a compliment."

He gave a chuckle. "I can tell you watched a lot of Disney as a child. You have an unnaturally positive outlook on life."

She brought his tea over with a smile. "Maybe. But it's served me well. Anyway, who says I ever stopped watching it?"

"You don't have a TV here."

"I wish I did. But alas… All these books are expensive. I used to watch on my laptop, but it's so old now, I can barely write my assignments on the thing."

"Huh." He sipped his tea, but his eyes never left hers. "Well. That's a shame."

"Yeah. Hey, do you mind if I get changed? I need to put on 5,000 layers of extra clothing if I'm gonna sit around in here."

"Go for it," he smiled. "You know, the boiler issue is pretty minor. I should be done in five minutes."

"Really?" She made her way over to the bed and switched on her Christmas lights. Then she began artfully arranging her screens for maximum privacy.

"Yeah. It's just the—"

"Don't tell me. I won't have any idea what it means."

"Fair enough," he laughed.

She watched for a moment as he grabbed a spanner from his toolbox before turning back to the boiler, his gaze intent. He was so fucking *focused*. Everything he did, he did completely. And she bet that intensity translated well to certain other areas of his life…

Biting her lip, Bailey shifted the last of the screens, hiding him from view. If she were acting like her mother, she'd take this as a golden opportunity and let him catch a glimpse here and there as she undressed; turn it into a dance of demure seduction.

But she was nothing like her mother. She remembered that as she turned her back on the silhouette of the man she was starting to want a little too much.

CASH TIGHTENED the last copper bolt before he set down his tools and leaned against the kitchenette's narrow counter. The knowledge that Bailey was undressing behind those bloody screens like some kind of Victorian lady sent a spark of heat to his gut that was even more intense in the frigid cold of her little flat.

And the sight of her shadowy outline was too fucking much.

He watched in strained silence as she undressed, despite the voice in his head telling him that he was crossing a line—that she certainly hadn't intended him to stand here and enjoy an impromptu show. But when the shadow that was Bailey began to peel her jeans off of her lush, rounded hips—when the silhouette of her thighs jiggled as she bent over—he lost the ability to control himself. Jesus, fuck.

Cash let his head fall back against the tiled wall. All his adult life, he'd been wary of desire. Of need. Of the addiction that one person could develop for another. And he'd thought that he danced with danger every time he took a woman to bed, because his need for touch was so strong, and because he worshipped each body so thoroughly.

He'd been wrong. He'd been so, so wrong. Cash had never been in danger of truly needing a woman.

Not until now.

He risked another glimpse at the screen and caught her in profile. Her hair must be hanging in front of her face, because he couldn't make out her features. But her body… he saw that well enough. Her tits were sweet little upturned mounds, barely there. He bet her nipples were stiff with cold. God, he'd warm her up, if he thought she'd let him. If he thought it was safe. If he thought a woman like her would accept the little he could give.

Her belly was soft and rounded, her waist thick. Her thighs were thicker, deliciously so. She bent over to do something—pull on some sort of clothing—and the plump curve of her arse almost tore a groan from his throat.

Cash closed his eyes. He had to, or he'd end up rubbing his hard dick through his jeans, and then he really would've gone too far.

But the darkness of his own mind offered no escape.

He strode forward and pushed the screen aside, finding her naked and gasping. His name crossed her lips, but he barely heard it—he was reaching for her, pulling her into him, his hands travelling over her shivering flesh like a tornado. First, he sank his fingers into the softness of her hips, her arse, revelling in their abundance; then he slid his palms up her ribs, cupped her little tits, brought each sweet nipple to his mouth in turn

—what colour would they be? His mind rushed to fill in the gaps—they were dark, so dark, like ink. He licked and sucked until she wept, until she clawed at him and begged for him and bloomed beneath his touch. And then he lay her down on the bed and plunged his aching cock into her slick heat, his body covering hers, her pussy pulling him deeper. But he looked into her lovely eyes and realised he hadn't even taken off her glasses—

"Cash?"

Her voice jolted him out of the fantasy.

"Yeah?" he called. Fuck. If he'd been hoping to hide the lust in his voice, he'd failed.

She sidled out from behind the screen, fully clothed. He didn't know if he should boo or cheer. She was wearing thick tracksuit bottoms and a huge, woolly jumper. Her feet were covered by fluffy, blue bed socks, and she was gathering her hair into a sloppy ponytail. She'd taken her glasses off for some reason, so she was squinting as she looked at him. And holy shit, she was beautiful.

"Do you want something to eat—?"

He crossed the room in two steps and took her in his arms. She had just enough time to let out a squeak of surprise before he brought his lips to hers. The need burning in his gut was fierce, but he forced himself to be gentle. She felt so soft; he didn't want to scare her. That was the last thing he wanted. And the way he felt right now was almost enough to scare *him*.

But God, this felt so fucking right. He feathered his lips across hers, once, twice, three times. Like falling snow. She let out quick little exhalations, and they tasted so sweet as they crossed his lips, dancing over his tongue. He slipped a hand behind her head, lost his fingers in the maze of her hair, and then—*there*. She softened. She melted.

For him.

Her hands came to his shoulders, light as butterflies. Fluttering, fluttering, nervously, until he pressed his mouth more firmly to hers, and then she moaned and held him tight, and he thought for the very first time that she might need him the way he needed her.

Fuck. *Fuck*. Her kiss was like a drug, and his heart rate was through the fucking roof, and was he really touching a woman like Bailey—a woman he wasn't prepared to let go, a woman he could never push away, a woman who wouldn't play by any of his rules?

Everything about her felt perfect. Not flawless; just exactly as God or whoever the fuck had intended. Perfect. For him.

But she *wasn't* for him. She couldn't be. Because Cash had a bad feeling that attempting anything other than forever with this woman would do nothing but fuck with his head.

What the hell was he doing?

Suddenly terrified, Cash pulled away. He watched as Bailey returned to reality, her pretty face creasing with confusion. God only knew what *his* face looked like, because his insides were a nest of vipers right now.

"Cash?" she said softly.

"I..." He searched for some way to fix the mess he'd just made, to reverse the process he'd just started. To stop himself from falling.

Too late. Gravity didn't work that way. And sometime in the last few minutes, this woman had become the centre of his solar system.

"I have to go," he said.

"Cash." Her voice hardened. "What the hell?"

"Your boiler's fixed." He turned to grab his tools, then abandoned the idea. No time for that. He had to leave. His mind frantic, he headed for the door.

"Don't," she said. "Don't be like this." Her voice didn't shake. He hadn't expected it to. One thing he'd realised by now: this princess was hard as fucking nails.

But diamonds were tough, too. And still precious.

"Bailey. Don't ask me to—"

"I've never asked anything of you and I don't intend to start." The words were sharp. "I'm *telling* you. Don't do this."

"I won't… I can't ruin you," he choked out, his back to her. His hand on the door. His heart in his mouth.

"There isn't a man on earth who could ruin me."

He believed her.

But obsession turned men into monsters.

"I'm leaving," he said.

And then he did.

CHAPTER 11

At precisely 10:30 the next day, Gem burst into the foyer wearing a flashing Santa hat and a long, silver beard.

"Santa! Is! HERE!" she boomed.

Bailey looked up from the book she was reading, blinking at the spectacle before her. There was a moment of silence. Then she said, "Your beard is falling off."

With a huff, Gem pulled down the elastic and let the long, silver curls hang around her neck. "The bloody thing's too big for my face," she griped.

"It looks better as chest hair anyway."

"Shut up. You are now my elf! Insubordination will not be tolerated."

With a resigned chuckle, Bailey slipped a pen between the pages of her book—*Sister Mine*—and pushed it aside. "I assume you have a task for me, then, Santa?"

"Indeed I do." Gem took off her rucksack and plonked it on the desk. It was partially unzipped, a profusion of scarlet and gold tinsel spilling from its depths. "Today, we decorate the office!"

"Oh, Lord."

"It'll be just like this." Gem swept her hand grandly about the room. "But *better*! Because I got *more tinsel*!"

The woman's enthusiasm was almost enough to make Bailey forget the dark cloud hanging over her head. Almost, but not quite. "Did you ask Cash about this?"

"No," Gem shrugged. "He won't care. He loves Christmas! Where is he, anyway?"

"He's not in yet." *Thank God.*

"Weird. Well, whatever. We can do it now! It'll be a surprise. Come on!"

"I don't think I should leave the phone…"

"It'll be fine! If anyone calls they can just leave a message." Gem skipped around the desk to grab Bailey's hands, dragging her up. "*Please*, please, please?"

An unwilling smile curved Bailey's lips. "*Fine.* But we have to be quick."

"Yay!" Gem turned to scurry up the stairs, her beard bouncing and her rucksack emitting suspicious jangling sounds.

With friends like this, who had time to waste thinking about confusing, arsehole men? Or their soft, wide mouths? Or the scruff of their stubble, or the heat of their big hands, or—

Oh.

Oops.

LIFE WAS full of little blessings. For example: having a whole morning free the day after you fucked up your chances with the sexiest woman on earth.

The Lord giveth, and the Lord taketh away. Not always in that order.

Cash had planned on sleeping in, but his brain wasn't down that with that idea. He hadn't had a wink of sleep all night, and the sunrise didn't make things any better; his mind was running like Usain Bolt on speed. Every time he closed his eyes, snapshots flashed up like something out of a film. Bailey. Bailey. Bailey.

He refused to draw her again.

But hanging around the house glaring at the furniture wasn't helping the situation. He needed to know how she felt. If she'd be furious or cold. Sharp or dismissive. The anticipation of pain was always worse than the pain itself, right?

So he decided to go to work early. He could get some admin done, anyway. He was being responsible, really. And he didn't have anything better to do.

Or anyone better to see.

But when Cash arrived at Fallen, his heart stuttering in his chest, he found the front desk empty. Suddenly terrified, he walked over, searching for some indication that Bailey had been here—that she was just out for an early lunch, or brunch, or some such nonsense—that she hadn't abandoned him completely. That he hadn't driven her away.

When he saw the book resting on the edge of the desk, he sighed with relief. Its cover was a psychedelic swirl of colour, interspersed with a guitar, a skull, and a pair of women who hovered like ghosts. He had no idea what the fuck it could possibly be about, but it was definitely the kind of thing Bailey would read.

Hope blooming from the wasteland in his chest, Cash headed up the stairs. She hadn't left. She wouldn't leave. He'd have a chance to fix this somehow—to take them back to the easy, unspoken attraction that had existed between them when she was just a barista and he was just a customer.

That old, simple sweetness had nothing on the memory of her lips beneath his. But it was a hell of a lot safer.

As Cash drew closer to the office, he heard voices: Gem's babbling chatter, the kind that came out when she was truly comfortable and carefree; Steve's wry mutterings, a little more confident than usual; and finally, Bailey's laughter. That was quickly becoming his favourite sound.

A grin spreading across his face, Cash pushed the door fully open and barrelled into the room.

Bailey was directly opposite him, facing the window, balanced precariously on his chair—his *wheeled* chair—as she wrapped a length of tinsel around the curtain pole. The chatter paused as Gem and Steve noticed his arrival, and the silence made her turn.

He knew exactly what would happen. He saw it all before his eyes like some kind of vision. And then, before he could do a damned thing about it, premonition became reality.

"Cash," she said, the same way you might say, *"Chlamydia?!"* after the doctor read out your test results.

And then she faltered, and the chair wobbled, and her feet got caught up in the stream of scarlet tinsel, and she fell.

Cash dashed across the room, mounting his desk in a leap he barely felt, so that he was kneeling on the scarred wood when Bailey landed squarely in his arms. Her hip slammed into his gut with enough force to knock the air from his lungs, and her outstretched arm smacked him square in the face, knocking little shreds of tinsel loose from the bunch she held in her fist. One gleaming, gold piece wedged itself between his lashes, irritating the fuck out of his eye.

But all he could do was stare down at her face. She was panting, gazing up at him with parted lips, and he thought he saw that look again. The look that said, *My hero*. And he'd been ready to see her pissed, or scathing, but not like this. He'd never be ready to see her like this.

His movements brisk, he pushed her off of his lap, holding her steady as she regained her feet. "You okay?" he asked tersely.

She nodded.

Cash blinked the tinsel out of his eyes and clambered awkwardly off the desk, glaring at nothing and no-one in particular.

Nobody spoke. Gem stared. Steve stared. Bailey looked firmly down at the floor. And Cash felt his temper flare.

"What the hell is going on in here?" he said tightly.

"We're decorating," Gem near-whispered.

Pinching the bridge of his nose, Cash took a deep breath. The last thing he'd ever do was shout at Gem for doing something he *wanted* her to do. But Jesus fucking Christ. His fury bubbling over, Cash turned on Steve.

"Why the fuck are you letting the girls climb on *chairs*?"

Steve held up his hands. "I wanted to help. But they wouldn't let me."

"We're not children," Bailey said, finally speaking. But her wide-eyed admiration was all gone. She was firmly back to disgust. "Steve doesn't *let* us do anything."

"Gem is an apprentice," Cash said, clinging to the edge of his patience. "You are a receptionist. *Steve* is a senior artist. And half a foot taller than both of you." He felt his voice rising to unacceptable levels; reigned it in; controlled the beast. His next breath felt like barbed wire dragging over raw skin. He took another. And another. When he spoke again, he sounded a hell of a lot calmer than he really was. "In future," he ground out, "*please* use a stepladder."

There was a pause. Gem said, clearly astonished: "We have a stepladder?"

With a groan, Cash threw up his hands and stalked out of the room.

So much for charming his way back into Bailey's good graces.

CHAPTER 12

Bailey hunched over her book, her eyes tracing a paragraph for the tenth time in as many minutes. Aside from a slight ache in her ankle, which she'd banged against the edge of Cash's desk, she'd suffered little from her fall earlier in the day. The worst-bruised thing was her pride.

And, apparently, her concentration.

"Hey, you."

She looked up to find Jay leaning against the front desk, his handsome face split into a grin. Great; she was supposed to be the receptionist, and she hadn't noticed him standing a foot away from her damned face. Excellent. Amazing. *Good work, Bailey.*

"What are you reading?"

"Um..." She closed the book and held it out to him. "*Sister Mine.*" Not that the *reading it* part was going too well.

"Huh." He turned it over to skim the blurb. "What's it about?"

"Demi-God twins. One of them has magic, the other one doesn't. The one without magic is being chased by a murderous spirit. And her sister is dating Jimi Hendrix's guitar." Jay didn't bat an eyelid. "It's set in Canada," she added.

"Weird," he said. He was studying the cover art with an expert eye. "This design is cool. It would work well for a tattoo."

"Maybe."

He handed the book back to her. "You don't have any tatts, do you?"

"I might. Where you can't see."

"You don't." His voice was sure. "I can tell. You're a virgin." He waggled his eyebrows.

"Behave yourself," she snorted. And then, warming to the topic: "I've been thinking about getting one for a while. I just don't know what I'd get."

"Your nan's birthday," he said dryly. "Universal starter tattoo."

She chuckled. "Not exactly what I had in mind. I'd like to lose my *virginity* with more of a bang."

And of course, at the worst possible moment, Cash appeared. He marched into the room with a scowl, the ink on his forearms shifting as he clenched his fists.

"What the hell are you two talking about?" he demanded.

Oh, crap. Bailey felt her cheeks heat—but Jay just slid an amused grin her way before turning lazily to face his boss. "Nothin'," he drawled.

"Jay," Cash said. His voice was rough as a mountaintop, hard as stone. Bailey thought she heard a thread of warning there—only that couldn't be right. Could it?

The men stared each other down like cowboys before a duel. The tension ratcheted up with each breath of silence. And then, just as Bailey's thoughts veered from confusion to concern, Jay broke out into laughter.

"Ah, come on man!" he cried, reaching forward to slap Cash on the shoulder. "I'm just fucking with you." Cash's face remained impassive, his broad frame unmoving. And yet, beneath his utter stillness, Bailey caught the impression of a rabid dog straining at the leash.

But Jay seemed blissfully unaware. He sauntered off into the studio, chuckling to himself, shaking his head. In the silence that remained, Bailey forced herself to meet Cash's eyes. He watched her like a hawk watches a mouse.

"We were talking about tattoos," she said, finally.

He shrugged those huge shoulders. "None of my business what you're talking about," he said gruffly. But she felt an urgent need to explain that… Well…

"I'm not a virgin."

He stared blankly.

"I'm, y'know—a tattoo virgin." She stretched her face into an awkward grin. "Haha!"

Cash didn't laugh. "I know that," he said.

"You do?"

"Of course." He finally moved, walking across the shop to look out of the high windows and into the street. His back to her, he continued. "Not your style."

She spluttered. "You don't know my *style*."

"Sure I do."

"No you don't," she insisted. And then, reckless indignation giving her that final push, she blurted out, "Actually, I want a tattoo."

He turned to look at her, arching a brow, and she fought the urge to squirm under the intensity of his gaze. "Do you, now?"

"Yes," she said firmly. *Maybe. Wait, no, definitely. Yeah.* The last of her reservations dealt with, Bailey nodded so hard that her glasses slipped down her nose. Blushing, she nudged them back up into place.

Cash wondered over to the desk with an ease that didn't quite match the fire burning in his eyes. When he rested his hands against the black wood, close enough to touch, she bit her lip. When he leaned forward, his long hair casting a shadow across his face, his lips close enough to bring back last night's awkward —*brilliant, beautiful, magical*—kiss, she gulped.

But she refused to look away.

"I didn't think tattoos were your thing," he said slowly.

She arched a brow. "I work here, don't I?"

"Not exactly through choice."

"If I didn't want to be here, I wouldn't be," she said.

"Tattoos aren't just about the thrill," he went on. "Body mods are a pretty fucking heavy commitment."

She gave his inked-up forearms a significant glance. "How ironic."

He inhaled sharply. A muscle leapt in his jaw, and she knew her hit had landed. *Good.*

But then, through gritted teeth, he fought back. "Whatever you might think of me, tattoos are my life. I've been working to succeed in this industry since I was a teenager, and every piece of art on my body means *something* to me. Might be significant; might just be the memory of a good day. It's enough, because I want them. Always. When times change, and even when *I* change, I want them."

Bailey stared, more than a little shocked by that speech, and he stared back, as though he couldn't believe he'd even said the words. As though he hadn't meant to. As though his passion had leapt ahead of his reason.

That seemed to happen to him a lot.

She liked it.

"Alright," she murmured. "I understand. But…I want one. I do. I want to—to *commit* to myself. For better or for worse." She shrugged. "Does that make sense?"

He paused, as if to let the words ruminate. And then, finally, he relented. "Yeah. That does make sense."

For some twisted reason, his approval sent a wave of satisfaction through her. He straightened up, turning to leave. "I'll do it."

Bailey frowned. "What?"

"Your tattoo. I'll do it."

"Oh, no," she spluttered. "That's not what I meant. I just wanted your advice. You can't do it. You're booked."

"Don't worry about that," he said, as though his waiting list wasn't months long.

"But—"

"Stay after closing tonight, okay? We'll have a little consultation."

"But—but I don't know what I want!"

"That's what the consultation's for."

"I can't afford you!"

He frowned. "Bailey. Don't be ridiculous."

"But—"

"After closing." And then he left.

Bailey huffed out her frustration, muttering her outrage to the empty room. The *audacity* of that man. He was so bloody high-handed it beggared belief.

So why was she fighting a smile?

CHAPTER 13

Perhaps she'd been a bit hasty.

Bailey could admit that. Not aloud, obviously, because Cash was sitting right next to her, smirking at the sight of her in the big old chair-bed thingy he tattooed people on. Probably still laughing at the fact that the straight-edge geeky girl in glasses thought she was cool enough for this.

Oh, whatever. She was just collecting trouble. Aside from his initial reaction, Cash had been entirely supportive. It was almost like last night had never happened. Almost.

"So what were you thinking?" he asked, his voice low, intimate. But that was just an illusion, because he'd made it quite clear that he didn't want to be intimate with her. Didn't want to *ruin* her, whatever that meant.

She'd always believed men should come with a warning label. It was rather accommodating of him to attach one of his own accord.

"Um..." She thought about the flash on the walls of the entrance room, of Gem's unique collection of tattoos, a scrapbook written across her skin. Of Jay's watercolour brights and Steve's traditional style. But before she could organise her thoughts, Cash turned and rifled in the shelves behind him, producing a slim sketchbook slightly smaller than his usual one.

He opened it at the first page and turned it around to face her. "What about something like these?"

She barely had the time to process the stylised, geometric drawing of—was that a badger?—before he flicked to the next one, where countless small illustrations were littered in a neo-traditional style. Dark quotes within sweet floral borders; a teacup that looked suspiciously like Chip from *Beauty and the Beast*, in which swirled a tempestuous storm. Then he turned the page again, and she gasped.

Somehow, with the harshest and darkest of shading, in a style that was all his own, he'd created the impression of luminous glass. It was a dome containing a single red rose, but the case was shattered. No; shattering, from the base up, cracks snaking along its smooth contours. Only the head of the lush bloom remained safe, and not for long. Some indefinable magic swirled around the image, a trick of light and shadow that only an artist could begin to understand, never mind wield.

She looked up at him, unable to hide her awe. "You did this?"

He nodded.

"For me?" But she already knew the answer. Of course it was for her. "How did you..." She trailed off, unsure of exactly what she was asking. How had he known—?

That I've been fascinated by the rose my whole life, by the ticking time bomb that lay between Beauty and her Beast. That I was still such a child on the inside, still so caught up in my past. That I'm ready to accept that, and own it, and etch it into my skin.

How did you know before I did?

But all she said was, "This one. I want this one."

"You sure? You don't want something smaller, for now?"

"I'm sure."

"Alright," he said, his voice gruff as he snapped the sketchbook shut. But he was pleased with her reaction; she could tell. He let his long hair fall into his eyes, and his lips curled slightly in something that was too soft to be a smirk.

"I know where I want it, too," she said.

"Ah, yeah; I was gonna ask. It's a big piece, or I'd like it to be."

"You'd like it to be?" She arched a brow.

"Yeah. I know exactly how I want every tattoo I create. Whether the canvas feels like cooperating is a different matter."

She laughed as she leaned back in the huge chair. That was the funny thing about being with Cash—no matter how on edge she felt at first, somehow she always ended up relaxed. Comfortable. Happy. Lord knew why. He was a grumpy fuck.

A grumpy fuck who'd spent half the day wearing Gem's flashing Santa hat. But a grumpy fuck, nonetheless.

"It would be interesting, getting into your head," she murmured. It was just a passing thought; one she had often, but not anything she thought would ever happen.

Yet he reacted like she'd tied him up and started an interrogation. Instantly, the light left his green eyes, as though clouds had passed over the quiet sunshine of his happiness. He stiffened, folded his arms, and the menacing combination of thick muscle and dark ink sent a thrill through her that wasn't entirely to do with the fight or flight response.

"Nothing interesting in my head," he said tonelessly. "It's a wasteland."

"You're an artist. That's impossible."

"Guess we'll never find out, then." His face might as well have been hewn from stone.

Bailey studied him for a moment, her curiosity well and truly piqued. But something about the set of his jaw, the brittle line of his broad shoulders, told her to change the subject.

"I was thinking my thigh," she blurted out. *Steamroller the conversation, and he'll forget it ever happened. Good one, Bailey.*

But it worked. He looked down at her bent leg as though she'd just kicked him in the face with it, blinking slowly.

"Right," he said. "Your thigh."

"Plenty of space, right?"

He muttered something under his breath. It sounded like *Hell, yeah.*

But he wouldn't make fun of her like that, would he? Cash had never seemed the shallow type. Then again... She remembered the woman from a couple of weeks back, the one who'd clearly had something more with him, once upon a time. She was a skinny thing. Model-like.

Bailey jumped as Cash's hand landed on her knee.

"Whatever you're thinking," he said firmly, "stop it."

"What?"

"I don't like the look on your face right now."

She bit her lip and she looked down at his hand on her. It was his left hand, un-inked, the skin pale against her dark blue jeans. She looked back up at him and their eyes clashed. Her body tingled as that familiar, indefinable heat grew between them, sparked by the raw, open look in his eyes.

"Bailey," he choked out. That was all. Just her name, his voice strangling the two syllables as though they were the hardest thing he'd ever had to say.

She tore her gaze from his, her pulse racing. Without her permission, her hands moved, and before she knew it her fingers were tracing the swirling lines of his octopus tattoo. His skin was hot, almost burning, and so soft despite the hard muscle beneath.

"Bailey," he said again. "Sometimes... Sometimes you look at me like..."

"Like what?" she asked when his voice trailed off.

"I don't know," he said finally. "I don't know how to describe it. But it makes me wish I were a better person."

She frowned up at him. "Why would you say that? You're wonderful." And as soon as the words left her mouth, she realised they were true. Despite everything between them, he was wonderful, in his way.

And so, when he leaned in close, a question in his eyes, she didn't protest. Instead, she reached up and took her glasses off, folding them carefully before putting them on the little table beside her. And then she turned back to Cash and curled her fingers in the fabric of his T-shirt, dragging him closer. Without her glasses, and with their faces so close, he appeared in gentle detail; beyond beautiful and beyond real. And he was here, with her. That was close enough to *being* hers. Wasn't it?

But wait—she didn't want that, anyway. She didn't want that at all. So she reached for what she did want. Arching up, Bailey brought her lips to his.

He may have been the one leaning over her, a hand gripping her thigh, the other cradling her head—but she was the one in control this time. She surrendered to the insistent thrum of desire that his presence roused, basked in his heat and the familiar smell of ink and paper and coffee that clung to him. Her tongue slid between his lips and she tasted him like he was a fine wine, locked away for decades, for *centuries,* in anticipation of this very moment. Because, Lord, it felt like she'd been waiting her entire life to kiss a man like Cash Evans.

No. Not a man like him.

Just him.

He groaned against her lips, and then she felt the huge chair shift as he climbed on, over her, his legs bracketing hers and his broad body covering her own. She arced against him and was rewarded when her pelvis met the stiff column of his erection, sending a delicious thrill through her veins. Desperate, thoughtless, wanting—her reality sharpened to a fine point in which nothing but need mattered. She rose up again, writhing beneath his wickedly decadent weight, grinding her aching pussy against his swollen cock.

"Oh, fuck," he moaned low into her mouth, and then his big hands skimmed their way up her torso, pushing her jumper up out of the way. He pulled back to gaze down at her exposed chest. She rarely bothered with bras. What was the point, when she had so little to fill them? Except now, she wished she had—a Wonderbra, perhaps, with a mountain of padding, so her breasts didn't look quite so small cupped in his big hands.

But then, he didn't seem to mind. He was gazing down at her with hunger in his eyes. He lowered his head to suck one stiff nipple, his tongue worshipping the tip even as his lips tugged, and suddenly she didn't give a fuck about the size of her tits. How could she, when he made them feel so fucking *good?*

She wrapped her legs around his narrow hips almost instinctively, her mind more animal than rational as lust took over. He reached down with one hand to grab her thigh, kneading the thick flesh as though he couldn't get enough, and she moaned his name like a prayer.

He released her nipple with a little *pop* that almost made her giggle, his thick stubble tickling her sensitive skin. But then she saw the deadly serious look on his face.

"What is it?" she whispered.

He studied her with something close to wonder in his eyes.

"I just… I never thought it would feel like this," he said. "You're so…"

She didn't wait to hear the end of his sentence. She didn't need to hear it. She didn't want to hear it. Because she'd heard it all before.

Her desire drained like blood from a wound. Her body stiffened beneath him, but he didn't seem to notice. Probably too busy dreaming up pretty speeches designed to talk her out of her knickers.

"You don't need to do that," she muttered.

He frowned. "Do what?"

"Talk all that fairytale bullshit to me." She pushed against his chest, not hard, but he pulled back as though he'd been burned, standing up before she could blink. Rearranging her clothes, Bailey stood too.

"Wait," he said, reaching for her—but she stepped smartly out of his way, and he let his hand fall. "What… what did I do?"

She squinted in the general direction of the side table,

fumbling for her glasses and trying not to knock any ink bottles over. Then she felt his hand close over hers as he passed them to her. Her jaw tight, she took the glasses and put them on. They were smudged, but she wasn't about to stand there and clean them.

"I'm not an idiot, Cash. I don't know how you usually operate, but you don't need to give me the Prince Charming speech if you want to fuck. Just ask. I'll give you a yes or no answer."

He raked his hand through his hair, and she was almost undone by his apparent frustration. Almost. "It wasn't a speech," he insisted, frowning in confusion. "I mean… What, you think I'm just making this shit up? You think the way I feel about you is fake?"

She smiled sadly. The way he *felt* about her? God, he was good. "When it comes to relationships, *everything's* fake. We all convince ourselves that lust has to mean happily ever after, or it doesn't count. And when you base one thing on a lie, everything that follows is false."

He folded his arms, his face hardening. "That's an interesting way of looking at things. But nothing about me is fake, Bailey."

"Careful," she said softly. "Don't make a liar of yourself." But then she shook her head, smiling at her own foolishness. "What am I saying? You can't help it. Everyone does. Eventually."

He came closer, his broad body looming over her, reminding her suddenly of how very large he was. "You want me," he said, his voice urgent, insistent.

"Obviously." She didn't step back, didn't cower. She had no need to. She wasn't afraid of Cash.

Just of the way he made her feel.

"So why are you putting up some bullshit barrier?" he demanded.

She set her jaw stubbornly. She was in the right. She knew she was. God—she'd watched enough films in her life to know a line when she heard one.

He shook his head at her silence, a mocking smile curving his lips. "Alright, then. I can give you what you want to hear." He bent over her, crowding her, until she finally felt the urge to step back, just to escape the intensity of his gaze. "I don't know how that romantic shit works. None of it. I don't know what I was thinking."

Though she'd suspected as much, the admission felt like a blow to Bailey's chest. But then he reached out, wrapped his long fingers around her forearms, and when he spoke again, his tone was almost desperate. "But *you,* Bailey—I want you. Badly. Except I can't fucking have you. Because all I've ever offered a woman is ninety days. A fling. Three months, at most, and I'm gone. No emotional bullshit, and no going back. It's all I'm good for and it's all I know." A sour smirk curved his lips. "You say you don't want fairytales—but I doubt you want that."

She swallowed, working hard to keep her face impassive. To keep the barrier erect. And if she thought she saw a glimmer of disappointment, of hopelessness, behind his tiger's eyes...

She was mistaken. She must be mistaken.

Bailey thought fast. His words were wreathed in challenge, and she knew what he thought. That she was a good girl. That she needed hearts and flowers or nothing at all. It never occurred to people that a woman might possess more than two dimensions. That she might be awkward, geeky, *and* horny all at once.

She reached out and put her hand against his chest, and enjoyed the flare of surprise in his eyes. "Actually, you're wrong. I'll take that. Happily."

His speechlessness was to be expected, but it was still bloody satisfying.

She turned to leave—but he pulled her back. Captured her by the wrist and tugged her to him and whispered, his voice raw, "Don't fuck with me, Bailey."

"I'm not," she said. "But I'd certainly like to fuck you."

She gave herself a second to enjoy the shock on his face before she walked out.

CHAPTER 14

Lust was nothing new to Cash.

How could it be? He was a man of intense appetites. Hence the strict time limits he placed on his relationships.

When he woke up on Sunday morning with a hard cock and a head full of Bailey, he wasn't surprised. He'd been dreaming of the damned woman for months now. It was almost embarrassing, at this point. And while he'd assumed that a taste of her would be enough to slake his thirst, that didn't seem to be true. Because since the moment he'd first kissed her, Cash's need for Bailey had been spiralling out of control.

That worried him. That worried him a lot.

And *now*—holy shit. Now she was, theoretically, within his reach. As long as she didn't change her mind.

Jesus Christ, he hoped she wouldn't change her mind. It might kill him.

As the early morning sun filtered through his pale curtains, Cash threw off his thick, winter duvet and exposed his naked body to the cool air. He wrapped a fist around his erection and stroked, fast and hard, memories flashing through his head.

Bailey, her head thrown back, her face a picture of agonised lust. Her body beneath his, the plump softness of her hips, the silky skin of her tits, those black-coffee nipples hardening between his lips…

Then the memories slowed. Changed. Became something else. Fantasies, things he'd never seen before.

Her naked body in his bed, relaxed and satisfied. Her hand in his as she smiled up at him, her brown eyes sparkling, her joy uncontrolled. Her fingers playing softly with his hair. He heard her voice whispering his name, and she sounded like she loved him.

Cash opened his eyes and sat bolt upright.

"What the fuck?" he murmured.

His phone rang.

It was her. It had to be. He reached over to the bedside table, answered the call with embarrassing eagerness. "Bailey?"

"It's John, idiot. Don't you have caller ID?"

Cash sighed, rubbed a hand over his face. Of course it wasn't Bailey. She'd never called him. "For fuck's sake. What time is it?"

"Obviously not too early for Bailey to ring you."

"Bailey's a lot prettier than you are."

"So you admit that you think she's pretty?"

Cash rolled his eyes and lay back against the bed, resigned to his doom. "I admit nothing. Did you call me for a reason?"

"I did, actually."

"Yeah? What?"

"I just wanted to let you know that you don't need to drag me to your mother's for Christmas anymore. Not that I don't appreciate the offer, because I do."

"Really? You got plans?" Cash had invited John home for Christmas after confirming that the other man had no family worth mentioning. John was settling into work well and they were looking into a flat for him, but he'd been set to spend Christmas alone. And Cash couldn't have that.

"Yep! This guy from work, Pete, he doesn't get on with his

family either. So we talked about it, and we've decided to spend Christmas together!"

Cash felt a suspicious smile curve his lips. "Really? That's very… neat."

"Yep!" John said brightly. "Just two loners joining forces!"

"Oh, that's what it is, is it?"

"Mmhm!"

"Right. So you're not interested in this Pete guy at all?"

"Umm…" The embarrassment in John's voice practically seeped through the phone. But then, after a pause, he said, "No more than you're interested in Bailey."

"I'm not—" Cash stopped, dragging a hand across his face. *Fuck*. "Did she… Did she say anything to you?"

"Nope," John said smugly. "But you just did."

"You little shit."

"Merry Christmas!" John put the phone down.

Ah, crap. Cash raked a hand through his hair, gazing at the soothing blankness of his bedroom ceiling. He could hear the faint notes of gospel music from the flat above. Mrs. Adebayo must be cleaning.

He should be pissed at John putting him on the spot. Instead, he was fighting the urge to grin like a sap. Which was bad. Very bad.

He was beginning to think that this thing with Bailey wasn't going to go like the rest of his… *relationships,* if they could be called that. Things weren't going the way they should. His feelings were too fast; everything else was too slow.

But maybe that was the problem. Maybe he was spending too much time in his own head. She was only a woman, after all; she was only human. And she'd agreed to his terms, even if he couldn't quite believe it.

If Cash stopped torturing himself with the idea of her, stopped putting her on some kind of pedestal and just *had* her…

Well. Then he'd have had her, wouldn't he? Past tense.

Done.

❄

On Monday morning, Cash arrived at the shop bright and early, more than ready to see the woman he'd spent his Sunday fantasising about. He parked his bike out the back, as always, and stamped carefully across the sheen of ice coating the carpark, his heart pounding almost as loud as his boots.

But he frowned as he approached the shop: it looked dark. The lights were off. And when he tried to open the door, it didn't budge.

Because it was still locked. Because Bailey didn't work Mondays.

Fuck.

The next day, Cash dragged himself in with fresh determination and no little frustration. And even though the lights were on, flooding the frozen street with warmth, and the door swung open when he pulled, he couldn't help but worry that she'd be absent. That he'd have to spend another day desperate to see her, to speak to her, choking on words that had no outlet.

But she was there, of course. Alone. Perched at the desk in one of her funny little Christmas jumpers, reading some huge book with tiny writing and lots of diagrams, a highlighter pen in her hand. She didn't look up as he came in. She simply became still, painfully still, and her eyes flicked over lines of text rapidly, and the luminous yellow pen she was holding bobbed up and down in the air.

Cash moved around the room, turning on all the Christmas lights. She didn't ask—didn't even acknowledge his presence—but he told her anyway.

"I like it when it's all lit up."

He thought she might not respond. But after a few moments, she murmured, "Okay." Softly, absently. As though she hardly cared either way.

But he knew the truth. She was nervous.

He walked up to the front desk, leaned against it, his forearms inches away from her book. "What are you reading?" he asked.

"*Brain Asymmetry and Neural Systems*."

"Sounds… hard."

She finally looked up, and her dark gaze felt like a punch in the gut. "It's fine," she murmured. "Not the worst thing I've had to read."

"Right," he said. "Listen—I wanted to talk to you."

She put her highlighter down in the middle of the book, then closed the pages around it. Resting her hands neatly on the desk, she straightened her spine, her eyes huge behind her glasses.

"You don't have to look so nervous."

"I'm not nervous."

"Alright."

God, they sounded ridiculous. Like strangers or business associates or anything other than two people who'd drowned in each other's air and loved it.

"Bailey," he began. "I really fucking like you." Not what he'd meant to say. But it was true, and it was too late to take it back, so he forged on. "And I'm sorry about the other night—if I did anything to make you uncomfortable. That's not what I want." He sighed, pushed a hand through his hair, his fingers itching for a pen. "You should know that if—if you want to change your mind, or you're not sure—"

"Not sure about what?" she said softly, cutting him off before he could ramble any further. "About us?"

He grimaced. "About my…. rules."

"That's what you call it?" Her smile was wry, teasing. She wrapped a loc around her fingers, and Cash was suddenly desperate to do the same. To touch her somehow, not in passion but in casual intimacy. As if he had the right.

Then, as though she'd heard his thoughts, she reached out and put her hand on his. Traced her fingers over the face of the moon etched into his skin. The simple touch was so achingly sweet, he found himself leaning forward until his forehead bumped hers, his eyes closed, his lips a breath away from their ultimate goal.

"I'm not some kind of princess," she whispered. "You don't have to treat me like one."

"Yes you are," he whispered back, "and yes I do."

"Fine. But princesses like no-strings sex just as much as the next girl."

Fuck.

Just like that, he was hard as a rock. And then Bailey pulled away, sliding off her stool, her brown eyes glittering. Hungry.

"Come round here," she said.

Well, shit. His cock straining against his jeans, Cash practically ran around to her side of the huge, high desk, his heartbeat pounding in his ears. He stood before her, the desk separating them from the rest of the world. With a mischievous smile, she pulled him closer.

Not by his hand. By his belt

"Sit," she said lightly, pushing him towards the stool she'd just vacated. And then, before he could follow her instructions—"Oh, but wait. Let's take these off first."

Cash watched in a daze as Bailey fucking Cooper, the woman he'd wanted for *weeks*, undid his jeans and pushed them down his thighs.

Was he high?

Under the guiding force of her hand, he finally sat, watching her watch his cock. He was embarrassingly hard, considering they'd been talking for all of ten minutes. And he didn't give a fuck; not when she stared down at his stiff length like it was everything she'd ever wanted.

Bailey sank onto her knees in front of him, her hands hovering just above his thighs, drawing closer and closer to his aching cock with every passing moment. He waited for what felt like a century as she studied him, a satisfied smile curving her lips.

She might be satisfied, but he wasn't.

Yet.

"Touch me," he choked out, his voice hoarse.

She looked up at him, arching a brow. "Where are your manners?"

A growl of frustration tore from his throat as he gave into temptation and sank his hands into her hair. *"Please."* He'd never begged a woman in his life. But whether she knew it or not, he was begging now.

"Alright," she whispered. He braced for the feel of her soft hands.

It never came.

She lowered her head, looking up at him over her glasses, and slowly ran her tongue from the root of his dick up to the swollen head. Cash hissed out his relief, his need, his desperation, through clenched teeth. He tightened his grip, lacing his fingers through the slender locks of her hair, pulling just a bit, showing her exactly what he wanted.

More.

Apparently, she was happy to oblige.

She gave him another hot, wet lick, and just as he thought he'd combust from the wanting, her plump lips finally slipped over the tip of his length. He felt her tongue swirling around his fevered skin, lapping up his pre-cum. She sucked him deeper, her cheeks hollowing, her eyes wide.

"Bailey," he growled, watching as she swallowed him whole. He hit the back of her throat, felt her gag, felt her get over it. Holy shit. Then she took him deeper, and he realised he'd said the words aloud—was still saying them, under his breath like a prayer. *"Holy shit, holy shit, holy shit..."*

She worked his shaft with her lush mouth, the pressure sending stars shooting through his mind. No dark thoughts now. No fucking thoughts at all. Just the sight of her coffee-coloured eyes, of Bailey on her knees before him in a fucking Christmas jumper, and the way he wanted to kiss her and come down her throat and hold her and fuck her senseless all at once—

The front door creaked as it swung open, and Cash almost died. He was certain of it. His spirit jumped right out of his body.

"Morning, boss!"

Gem was standing in the doorway, stamping icy mud onto the welcome mat, her gaze blessedly focused on her precious, pink Doc Martens.

Cash stood up, sat down, stood up, remembered that the desk was high enough to hide Bailey—and his naked erection—and settled for leaning against its surface with what he hoped was nonchalance. By the time Gem looked up, her smile bright as always, the orgasm that had been racing towards him like a freight train had come to a screeching halt.

"Hey, Gem!" he said, and shit, was that too… jovial?

Apparently so. Gem paused in the act of unzipping her coat, giving him a quizzical look. "Are you okay?

"Um…"

"What are you doing down here, anyway? Where's Bailey?"

"I'm here!" Bailey breezed, popping up from beneath the desk like a fucking daisy. His wilting dick was still wet from her lips, and she was smiling and nudging up her glasses like nothing had happened.

"What were you doing down there?" Gem frowned.

Cash almost choked.

"Dropped a pen," Bailey said, sauntering out from behind the desk. "Cash is just checking the booking spreadsheet I made."

Gem wavered for a moment. He could almost see the indecision on her face. The woman knew him well enough to realise he wanted Bailey, that was for sure—but she also knew Bailey. Sweet, sensible Bailey.

Bailey Cooper would never suck her boss's cock behind the reception desk, would she?

In Gem's mind, apparently not. Because her face cleared and she said, "Oh, you did one? I was supposed to do that. But I didn't."

Bailey laughed along with her. "I don't blame you. It was a pain in the arse. But I've been meaning to talk to you about the wreath we put over Jay's desk…" She led Gem off towards the stairs, nattering away about the Christmas decorations in the office.

But then, just when he thought he'd have a few precious minutes to pull up his damn jeans, Bailey paused. There was a teasing glint in her eye as she called over her shoulder, "Oh—your one o'clock had to cancel. He wanted to know when you're next available for a two-hour session."

He waited for her to continue.

She didn't.

"And you said?" he finally gritted out.

"That he should call in the new year, when we start the next cycle."

"Good."

It was a method they'd devised a while back, after the books began to fill up months in advance. They only accepted appointments in three-month cycles: the books opened once every quarter, and that was that.

"He was pissed."

"I'm sure he'll live." *But I might not if you don't get Gem out of here before anyone else arrives.*

Her amusement written all over her face, she turned and continued towards the stairs. Then a thought hit, and Cash found himself calling after her, nudity be damned.

"Hey. Do you want to take my one o'clock?"

She looked back. "What?"

"Your tattoo. Want to do it today?"

He held her gaze steadily, letting her see the dare in his eyes Expressions flitted across her face: surprise, hesitation, wariness, and then defiance.

"Okay," she said finally. "Sure. Whatever."

He arched a brow.

"I said yes," she snapped, glancing pointedly at Gem, and then at the door. Oh, *now* she cared about his cock swaying in the wind.

"Alright then," he smirked. "I'll hold you to that."

She scurried off up the stairs, dragging a baffled Gem behind her.

CHAPTER 15

Sweet Baby Jesus in a manger, why the fuck had she said yes?

She must have been light-headed. From standing up too fast. Or choking on Cash's absurdly beautiful dick. One of those. Bailey lay back against the huge leather chair where she'd been rather wonderfully ravished just a few days ago. Before she'd ruined the moment, that is.

Now her skin was tingling, her face was warm and her heart was pounding, but there was nothing wonderful about it. She was absolutely shitting herself.

Gem stood over her, looming like a fuchsia-haired ghost. She was chewing on some obnoxiously bright Hubba-Bubba, pausing every few minutes to blow an acid-green bubble. "You nervous?" she asked.

"No," Bailey said. She heard Cash snort and turned sharply to look at him—but he was bent over his tattoo gun, his face blank. *Hm.*

"She's bricking it," Jay chuckled from a few feet away, working on a client of his own. The client, a huge bald guy with a long, white beard, was having his bare belly tattooed, a concept which made Bailey's own stomach tighten reflexively. That had to hurt.

But he was grinning merrily. "Don't worry, m'duck," he said in a broad, local accent, the kind her grandmother had spoken in before she'd died years ago. "Y' be alright." He gave her a wink.

She smiled weakly back at him. "Thanks."

"Okay," Cash said at last. He'd been fiddling at his little station for a good ten minutes now, and her anxiety had built with each second. "Take 'em off." He nodded down at her jeans.

She stared at him, aghast. "Oh my God, no."

"Bailey," he said patiently. "While I have many talents, I cannot tattoo you through denim."

Of course he couldn't. What was wrong with her? She'd been so worked up over the pain, and whether she was about to cry like a little girl and embarrass herself, the practicalities had completely slipped her mind.

"I—I just... I forgot you'd have to... Oh, God."

He chuckled, shaking his head. "It's alright. We'll draw the curtain."

"Do you want my hoodie?" Gem asked brightly. "To go over your—"

"Yes! Please!"

Gem gave Cash a look. "Bugger off, then. Let us get ready."

"Must I?" he sighed dramatically. But he was already standing up. He drew the curtain around their little area, shutting himself and everyone else out. Bailey could still hear the buzzing of Jay's tattoo gun, and the subtle aggression of the sound had nerves coiling in her gut like a pile of worms.

"Come on," Gem said briskly, pulling off her hoodie.

"Oh, yeah." Bailey stood and unbuttoned her jeans, beginning the rather awkward process of peeling the stretch-denim from her thighs. "Thanks so much, Gem."

"No worries. But you won't be able to put those on after, you know."

"Oh, crap."

"I'll nip out to the shops and get you something."

"You're a lifesaver." Bailey freed herself from the jeans and straightened up, folding them neatly. At least she had on decent underwear.

"What size are you?"

"Eighteen. On the bottom, anyway."

"Cool."

Bailey sat back against the huge seat, and Gem bustled around her, arranging the hoodie over her lap so that only one thigh was exposed.

"Alright," she called after a few final tucks. "We're decent!"

"Bailey might be," Jay called back, "but you aren't."

"Hilarious." Gem rolled her eyes as Cash stepped back through the curtain. "I'll be off, then. Won't be long."

"Okay," Bailey said. Her voice was unnaturally high and strained. She cleared her throat and offered Gem a tight smile. "See you in a bit."

"See you!" In a flash of grey, plastic-y curtain, Gem was gone.

Cash sat beside her once more, his eyes tender. "You okay?" he asked.

"Yeah."

"Nervous?"

"Maybe. A little bit." She thought for a second. "Do you think we could open the curtain now? So I have something to distract me?"

"Of course," he said softly. He pushed the curtain back, bringing Jay and his bearded client into view again.

"This your first one, is it, love?" the man asked.

"Yeah," Bailey said. Had breathing always been this hard?

"Bit nervous, are ye?"

She jumped as Cash pressed a piece of transfer paper to her outer thigh. "Um. A little bit."

"Just got to get on with it, that's all, my darlin'!"

Cash touched her forearm. "How's that?" he asked, nodding towards at her lap.

She looked down and found the rose design she'd loved so much, blown up and covering her leg in dark blue ink. A slow smile spread across her face as she studied it, and her clamouring nerves quieted, just a touch.

"That's great," she said. "Perfect."

"Good." He picked up his tattoo gun and switched it on. The menacing buzz sent her anxiety through the roof again. "I'm just going to do a little line, okay? So you know how it feels."

"Okay," she murmured.

"Don't look," Jay told her from across the room. "It's better if you don't look. You might be a bleeder."

Great.

Bailey stared up at the ceiling and focused on the music coming in from the entry room. It sounded like Ariana Grande, which meant Gem had got ahold of the sound system again. Not that Bailey was complaining. She loved *Christmas and Chill.*

She let the silky vocals rise above the buzzing tattoo gun in her mind, then took a deep breath. Which filled her nose with the comforting scent of Cash's soap, or shampoo, or whatever it was that made him smell like summer linen.

He put the needle to her skin.

It didn't hurt that much. Actually, she wasn't sure if it hurt at all.

He pulled away, looked up at her. "Alright?"

"Yeah," she said slowly. "It's… not too bad."

He grinned. "That's my girl." Then he bent his head over her thigh again and put the gun to her flesh.

She gazed up at the ceiling once more. Now that this was actually happening, she felt kind of silly. She could *feel* the needle, sure, but not enough to describe it as pain. It was like being prickled by a very persistent kitten: more shocking than agonising.

In fact, she'd been more disconcerted by the sight of Cash's head so close to her—

"Done!" Jay said, his voice rising in satisfaction.

"Cheers mate. Cor, that's somethin', eh?"

Bailey looked over to find Jay grinning at his client's round belly. Except, through abstract shapes and colours, it had been transformed into a… fishbowl? Bulbous goldfish chased translucent bubbles across the man's swollen skin. Bailey stifled a giggle as Jay began to wrap clingfilm over the fresh ink.

"You're so talented, Jay," she said, unable to keep quiet. Cash, it seemed, had no such concern; he was singularly focused on his work, silent as a church. But hey; she should be glad he was concentrating so hard, right?

"Thanks, Bailey," Jay smiled. "You're a sweetheart."

"I wish I could have colours like that," she mused. "But I'm probably too dark for it to show up."

Abruptly, Cash raised his head, pulling the gun away. "Wouldn't say you're *too* anything. You're the perfect natural canvas for all my heavy, negative-space stuff. It's like you were made for…" He trailed off, cleared his throat. "For my work," he finished. Then, just as suddenly, he bent back over her leg and started up again.

Bailey stared at the top of his head, coppery strands glinting under the fluorescent light. Then she looked up to find Jay and his client staring too, with similarly stunned expressions.

"He never talks while he's working," Jay said finally. "I didn't even know he… processed words when he was working. It's always like he's in some kind of trance."

"Aye," the big man agreed, sliding his T-shirt on. "He is a silent bastard, ain't he?"

"Usually," Jay muttered. Then he shook his head slightly. "Anyway, Lee, let's have you. Come on, mate."

They left the room, the client—Lee—giving her a cheery wave as he went. And then Bailey was alone with the *silent bastard.*

She waited for him to speak. To say something that would explain the aberration that had apparently just occurred.

But he didn't, of course.

God, where the hell was Gem?

CHAPTER 16

He should've known that things would be different with Bailey.

Weren't they always?

Cash had finished the last of the shading without an ounce of his usual peace. Working on Bailey, he hadn't been able to slip into a familiar state of euphoria, to float away until nothing mattered but his hands and the skin beneath them.

Nope. She kept him right there. Painfully present. Painfully aware. Bailey Cooper wasn't just a canvas.

He really should stay away from this woman, shouldn't he?

He was sitting in the corner of the room, watching everyone else crowd around Bailey as she admired her fresh ink in the mirror. Gem had provided her with a long, flowing skirt, which she hiked up around her thighs.

Jay, Steve, and Gem were all gushing over the tattoo—and he supposed he'd done a damned good job on it—but all Cash could focus on was the shape of Bailey's legs; the rounded curves of her thick calves and thicker thighs.

One of which was now marked forever. By him.

Abruptly, Cash stood. The sudden movement had all eyes

swinging his way. He cleared his throat. "We need to get that covered up."

"Alright," Bailey said with a smile. She hadn't stopped smiling since he'd finished, and her excitement was catching. It filled his chest like a balloon, made him want to cup her face and kiss her nose and—ugh. What the fuck was wrong with him?

He stalked forward and picked up the clingfilm, tearing off a length with a sharp pull. She sat for him, and he wrapped her up, his fingers lingering against the softness of her skin. It was way too late to pretend indifference. She knew what he wanted. Or he thought she did—but recently, *he* wasn't even sure what he wanted.

She was singing under her breath, a tune light as air. He stilled, straining to hear the lyrics.

"But why should I try to resist when, baby, I know so well... I've got you under my skin?"

Her voice was husky and weak and beautiful. As the familiar refrain trailed off, he looked up, right into the heat of her gaze.

"Thank you," she said softly. "I love it."

He nodded stiffly, unable to speak around the lump in his throat.

"Alright young'ns," Steve said. "That's enough faffing about for one day. I know we've all got plenty to do."

"Barely," Gem said, rolling her eyes. "We close tomorrow, anyway." But she and Jay dispersed obediently. Steve's dad tone could not be denied.

"What are you guys doing for Christmas?" Jay asked, cleaning up his station.

"Going to my brother's house and pretending his children belong to me," Gem said dreamily.

"Because that's not creepy at all."

"He has five kids! No-one needs five kids. He can definitely share."

Jay snorted. "What about you, Bailey?'

Cash watched as Bailey bit her lip, her face hesitant. Which was odd. She loved Christmas.

But then she said, "I'm… It's just me this year."

Awkward silence.

"Oh," Gem said finally. "Oh, that's rubbish. You don't have any family you can—?"

"No." Bailey straightened her skirt and stood, forcing Cash to step back. He watched as she fiddled primly with the cuffs of her jumper, keeping her eyes to the ground. Maybe that was enough to hide the sadness that surrounded her from everyone else in the room.

But not from him.

"You should come home with me," he said.

Wait.

Wait.

Had he just said that?

Shit.

She looked up at him, her brow furrowed. "With you?"

Clearly, he had indeed just said that. And he kept on saying it, like his mouth had been possessed. "To my mother's house. That's where I spend Christmas. With my sister and brother-in-law. They have two kids. I don't know if you…" He became suddenly aware of the silence in the room, of everyone's eyes drilling curious holes into his back. He felt the tips of his ears heat up, which just made the whole situation even worse. He was *blushing*, for Christ's sake, like a teenager. He didn't think he'd ever been so embarrassed in his life. What the fuck was he thinking, inviting Bailey to his *mother's* house? This wasn't part of the arrangement they'd barely begun. This wasn't his way. It certainly wasn't what she'd agreed to—

"I'd love to," she said. The words ran into one another, as though she'd blurted them out without thinking, which was a habit of hers. He loved that habit.

Especially right now.

"Really?"

"Yes. Definitely. I mean—thank you. For inviting me. Oh, only if you're sure! I don't want to intrude." Her smile faded, and he watched doubt take its place. That killed him.

"I'm sure," he said firmly. *Shouldn't be doing this.* "Extremely sure." *It's a bad idea.* "I want you to come." *In more ways than one.*

"Oh." Her smile returned, light as a bird on a bare winter branch. "Okay."

"I'm leaving on the 23rd. Get back on the 26th. That okay with you?"

"Yeah. Where is it?"

"Oh, not far. Just out of the city. But she likes us all to stay, and my sister comes over from Derby."

"Okay. Cool. Um… Thanks again. For the tattoo." She moved past him with a pleased little expression on her face that made him want to pick her up and hug her. Maybe he would. Except—

He turned, suddenly remembering the presence of the rest of the room. His staff stood, gawping openly. "Don't you fuckers have shit to do?" he snapped.

Jay shot him a smirk. "Aye aye, boss."

Cash raked his hand through his hair and stifled a sigh. He'd never hear the fucking end of this.

CHAPTER 17

Cash's family lived in a fantasy world.

Or at least, that's how it felt.

They'd driven to the outskirts of the city in a car she hadn't known he owned. It was small and dark blue and old-fashioned —vintage, clearly, but she had no idea about that sort of thing.

He kept on driving as they left the concrete jungle behind. Cityscapes became snow-cloud skies and barren fields. They passed winter-bare trees, their branches spearing up towards the heavens like needy hands raised to the gods.

The roads grew thin, winding through the landscape like ribbon. The foliage ripened again as evergreens took the place of deciduous plants. They passed a sign that read: *Welcome to Cartham,* and houses came into view, settled comfortably into vast plots of land along one side of the road. On the other side there stood what could only be called a forest, the trees as dense and erect as an army's front line.

Bailey raised her brows. "This is where your mother lives?"

"Yep." He slowed the car down as they pulled up to a set of huge, open gates. They swung into the brick driveway and crawled up towards a grand house of grey stone, its garden festooned with gaudy, flashing Christmas lights that contrasted boldly with the austere vibe of the area. It was like seeing a blow-up snowman and *Santa Stop Here!* sign in front of Northanger Abbey.

"You're not the only one who likes Christmas," she observed with a smile.

"No," he said as he pulled up. "I'm not. Listen, Bailey... Just to warn you, my mother thinks that you're my girlfriend."

"What?!" she squeaked, her smile disappearing. "Why?!"

He winced, clearly uncomfortable. This explained why, as they'd drawn closer to their destination, he'd gone from laughing with her over their disparate music tastes to falling into a brooding silence. He was nervous.

"Well," he said. "I told her you were coming. And she asked me about you, because she wanted to get you a present—"

"A present? Oh my God, she didn't need to do that!"

"She loves getting presents. The more the merrier. So I told her about you, and she kind of decided you must be my girlfriend."

Bailey squinted at him. "Why? What did you say?"

"Nothing, really. I told her your name. How we met. The stuff you like. I don't know, normal shit."

"Well, maybe it's just wishful thinking on her part. Don't mothers always want their sons coupled up?"

"Maybe," he agreed. "I just wanted to warn you. She's kind of enthusiastic. And I don't want you to feel pressured or—"

"It's okay," she said gently. "I know what this is, Cash." Even though he hadn't touched her since that day at work. Even though he'd asked for her number and done nothing with it but text her cute dog pictures. Even though they were sitting outside his mother's house right now.

She wouldn't allow herself to forget. *Ninety days.*

His hands were wrapped tightly around the steering wheel despite the car being stationery. She reached forward to cover them with one of her own. "Relax. It'll be fine."

He looked at her with those piercing eyes, so well-suited to this green little village, and she saw vulnerability in their depths.

"What are you so worried about?" she asked softly.

He heaved out a sigh. "It's hard to explain. But my mother, and my sister... We've all been through a lot together. They really mean the fucking world to me. And they think of me in a certain way—the wrong way. They're determined to see the best in me. Maybe it's selfish, but I don't want anything to change that. I need them to believe that I'm... like them."

"Like them?"

"Yeah. Like them, and not like my..."

He looked ready to choke on his words. His knuckles were white, the tendons of his hands raised beneath her fingers as he gripped the wheel.

"Like your father?" she guessed.

He looked at her sharply. "How did you—?"

"Generally it's our parents who fuck us up. And clearly you have no problem with your mother."

"Right." He took a deep breath. "Yeah. My dad was kind of shit. God, I don't know how to say this."

"You don't have to tell me," Bailey said softly, silently willing him to look at her again. But she wasn't ready for the agony in his eyes when he did.

"This isn't really the time. It's heavy, I suppose. He was... evil." Cash's voice turned to stone on that single word, something shadowed in his eyes. "Everyone said, when I was a kid, *you have to talk about it,* but I don't know why. My mum made me, uh, see a therapist. Fuck. That sounds weird, doesn't it?"

She smiled gently. "I study cognitive psychology, remember? Taking care of your mental health isn't *weird* to me."

He tried to laugh. It almost sounded like the real thing, too. " Well... Long story short, I've spent my life trying not to be like him. But sometimes I worry—"

Before she could find out what Cash worried, the front door of the house opened. Light spilled out into the growing darkness of the afternoon, and Bailey knew that the swirling concern in her gut would have to wait.

A woman stood in the doorway, tall and broad, a child perched on her hip—despite the fact that the kid must have been six or seven. Another child barrelled out from behind them, older than the first.

"Uncle Cash!" he roared, so loud they could hear him from inside the car. Cash gave her one last, long look before he opened the door and got out, sweeping the kid up into his arms.

"Hey, kiddo," he grinned, and there was pure love in his voice.

Bailey gave herself a second to fiddle with her hair. Just one. Then she put on her big girl knickers and got out of the car.

The air was icy cold, a slap in the face that made her giddy because it meant Christmas was coming. Of course, it would still be this cold after Christmas—in January, and February, and probably even March—but there wouldn't be magic in the air anymore. Not like there was now.

She let her excitement fill her, lift her up. Never mind her nerves, or the things Cash was trying to say, or the fear that shot through her every time his smile made her happier than it should. It was Christmastime. Nothing truly bad could happen.

Could it?

She was jolted from her reverie when Cash laid a hand on her shoulder. He smiled down at her, his big body protecting her from the wind. The boy in his arms had rich, brown hair and blue eyes, but his sharp features and petulant mouth were like distant echoes of Cash's own.

"Will, this is my friend Bailey. Bailey, this is Will, my eldest nephew."

"Hello," the boy said, his tone curious. He was wearing pyjamas and a thick, blue dressing gown. Batman slippers adorned his feet.

"Hi," Bailey said, soft and uncertain. She couldn't remember the last time she'd talked to a kid. But this one didn't seem so terrifying.

Cash gave a theatrical groan, sagging with fake weariness. "God, Will, you've grown so much I can barely carry you. I'm gonna have to put you down."

"No, Uncle Cash!" The boy bounced and giggled, kicking his legs. "Not yet!"

"Oh, alright then." Cash looked over at Bailey, and his smile was so wide and unguarded and real, she couldn't help but smile back. "Come on," he said. "I'll grab our stuff later."

They walked towards the front door, little Will talking a mile a minute about school, the pancakes he'd made earlier that day with his grandmother, the presents he thought he might get.

As they neared the house, Bailey felt herself falling behind Cash, her gaze lowered. Accepting his invitation was one thing, but now that she was actually here, it hit her how much of an outsider she was. An intruder. Fuck. She almost certainly should've stayed home.

Cash stepped into the house and put his protesting nephew down so that he could greet the woman who'd opened the door. He pulled her into a huge bear hug, lifting her off her feet—along with the little boy in her arms, who squealed excitedly. Bailey stood awkwardly aside, taking in the hallway.

It was light and airy, decorated in warm neutral tones and covered in Christmas decorations, just like the front of the house. Mistletoe hung over every doorway she could see, and tinsel was wrapped around every inch of the bannisters, trailing up the long staircase.

"Bailey," Cash said, capturing her attention again. "This is my sister, Monroe, and my other nephew, Charlie. Guys, this is my friend Bailey."

"Hi," Bailey said, trying her best to smile. She stepped forward, meaning to shake Monroe's hand, but at the last minute she realised that the woman's right arm was wrapped around her kid.

"Nice to meet you," Monroe said, her voice warm. She gave

Bailey a half-hug with her free arm, kissing her cheek. "This is momentous day! I had no idea my brother had friends."

Bailey laughed, her unease melting away at the warmth in Monroe's ocean eyes. The tall woman was solidly built, with pink, freckled cheeks and ginger hair shoved up into a messy bun. "*Friends* might be overstating it. We're more acquaintances, really."

"I knew it," Monroe chuckled. "Say hello, Charlie."

"Hello," the little boy said shyly. He was the spitting image of his brother, on a slightly smaller scale.

"Hi," Bailey smiled. "I like your slippers."

He looked down at the Thomas the Tank Engine footwear, a scowl on his face. "They're *old*. Grandma didn't get me new ones."

"Oh dear," Bailey murmured.

"Charlie! Don't be so rude." Monroe put the boy down with a huff, rolling her eyes. "He's worn out. My mum's had them doing all sorts. Anyway, come in, won't you? Let's get out of the hall."

The boys ran off into one room together while Monroe led Bailey and Cash into another. They stepped into a large, warm kitchen, at the centre of which stood an island piled high with food. A plump little woman with a cloud of ginger hair was bent over a huge, turquoise Aga, muttering curse words to herself and stirring a large pot.

"Mum," Monroe called. "Look who's here."

The woman turned, revealing a soft, weathered face creased with laugh lines and crow's feet. She wore an apron printed with holly and her sleeves were rolled up past her pink elbows. A wide grin split her face, revealing a gold tooth just behind one canine, and her eyes glinted a familiar green as she rushed forward.

"Cash!" she cried, her arms outstretched.

"Alright, Mum." He pulled her into a tight hug, lifting her up, and her little legs waved in the air. Then he set her down and she began smothering him with kisses, dragging his head down to her level with both hands.

"Look at your hair!" she cried. "You swore to me you'd get it cut for Christmas!"

"Forgot," he mumbled. "New Year's, yeah?"

"When will you shave this awful beard?"

"It's not a beard, Mum."

"I've no idea why you keep this scruff. You've a lovely chin, you have. You could be a model, you could! I don't know why you hate your dimples so much." Cash's mother appeared to be slightly deaf. Her every utterance was at least ten decibels louder than necessary. But Bailey couldn't bring herself to mind.

Then the older woman turned to Bailey, her gaze inquisitive. "And this is your *friend!*" she trilled. "How lovely! What a very pretty friend she is." She pulled Bailey into a hug that smelled strongly of ginger and syrup and face powder. "I'm Karen. Now, please make yourself at home, sweetheart. I want you to be perfectly comfortable, I do. Oh, bugger." She hurried back towards the Aga, where the pot she'd been stirring was threatening to bubble over. "I'm making spaghetti!" she cried. "Your favourite, Cashew Nut!"

"Mum," Cash sighed. "Could you please not—"

"Oh, yes! I'm sorry. I don't want to embarrass you in front of your *friend* now do I?" She gave him a theatrical wink. "Is spag bol alright with you, Bailey darling? You're not a vegetarian, are you?"

"Oh, no," Bailey reassured her, still trying to hide her smirk at the nickname *Cashew Nut*. "Spaghetti sounds great."

"Not gluten intolerant, are you?"

"Um, no."

"Not on the Atkins?"

"No?"

"The 5:2?"

"Mum," Cash interjected. "She's not on any kind of special diet."

"Oh, good! Good! I mean, I made spare food just in case. I

wasn't sure! Anyway, dinner won't be long, but there's snippets if you're hungry, loves." She waved vaguely at the island.

It was piled high with a buffet of food, from pigs in blankets on a hotplate to foil hedgehogs stabbed with pineapple and cheese cocktail sticks. Monroe leant at one end, munching on a cracker.

"We won't be able to eat all this, Mum," Cash laughed. "You must know that."

"Rubbish," Karen cried. "Nonsense! You're a big strong boy! It's Christmas! I got you some Terry's Chocolate Oranges, Cash my love, they were on offer at Sainsbury's. Do you like Chocolate Oranges, Bailey?"

"I do, Karen." Bailey grinned, thoroughly enjoying herself. This was like something out of a film; like the kind of mother she'd dreamt of as a kid, someone soft and warm and silly and sensible all at the same time. Like Molly Weasley, or something. Only she felt disloyal for thinking such thoughts, as though her own mother hadn't been good enough. She shook her head, pushed the pang of disquiet away.

"Excellent!" Karen was saying. "Wonderful! I was hoping you might, so I got plenty. I got After Eights as well, just in case you were a mint girl."

"I'll have any kind of chocolate," Bailey admitted.

"Oh, don't tell her that," Monroe warned. "We'll be rolling you out of this house by the time Christmas is over."

"Cash," Karen said suddenly. "What on earth are you still doing here, boy! Bugger off, will you? Go and see to your nephews. Or find George. He's here somewhere on one of his bloody computers."

"My brother-in-law," Cash said to Bailey with a wry smile. "Will you be okay, if I…?"

"Be off with you!" Karen insisted. "We're not going to eat her. We want some girly time, don't we Bailey?"

"Um…"

"Don't worry," Monroe grinned. "I'll rescue you if she gets carried away."

Bailey gave Cash a reassuring smile. "I'll be fine," she said softly. But he reached out and caught her hand in his, pulling her to him. Her heart leapt at the contact, the casual intimacy, the concern in his eyes.

"Are you sure?" he murmured, leaning over her. "I'll stay if you want me to."

"Honestly, it's okay." And it really was. She felt as though she'd fallen down the rabbit hole and ended up in the very best of Wonderlands. And the way his big, warm hand felt in hers… That was something she could get used to.

Just like all of this.

"Alright," he relented. He moved to leave, but at the last moment he turned back and pressed a swift, light kiss to her forehead. She stood and watched him walk away, her heart threatening to float right out of her chest.

She had no idea what was going on with that man. But she was starting to like it.

She turned back to Karen and found the older woman giving her a knowing look, her cheeks plumped by a smug smile. "You've softened up my boy," she said, speaking at a normal volume for the first time.

Bailey felt herself blush. "Oh, no, I just—I work with him. I mean, he was kind enough to help me out when I… Well—"

"Never mind all that," Karen said. "I know my little Cashew Nut. He's a funny boy, and he doesn't know where his own head's at half the time. But I know." She nodded wisely, waving the wooden spoon in her hand from side to side. "Oh, yes! A mother always knows!"

"Mum," Monroe said, coming to join them at the Aga. "Leave Bailey alone. I'm sure she and Cash are just friends."

Bailey sent the other woman a look of gratitude.

"I'm also sure that my brother would jump in front of a speeding train to protect your cat—do you have a cat, Bailey?"

"Um... No."

"Your dog? Guinea pig? Goldfish? The house spider under your bed that you've grown strangely fond of?"

"Ah..."

"What I'm *trying* to say is, he's smitten." Monroe smirked. "I'd be concerned if it weren't obvious that you are too."

"Oh, Roe!" Karen cried, whacking her daughter's backside with a tea towel. "You're awful! You're terrible! And you think *I'm* a problem! Leave the poor girl alone. Get her some wine!"

"*You* want some wine, you mean."

"Behave yourself, child! You're not too big to go over my knee, you know."

Bailey might be utterly mortified, but that couldn't stop her from laughing hysterically at the women's antics.

In fact, over the course of the night, she learned that laughter came easy in this house.

CHAPTER 18

Bailey didn't meet Monroe's husband, George, until they all sat down for dinner an hour later.

Monroe and her mother led Bailey into the dining room before setting the table together, moving like two halves of one whole in a choreographed dance. Monroe would carry a steaming dish, raising it high as the shorter Karen swept past her and back into the kitchen. Karen would pour Bucks Fizz with a practiced hand, swinging artfully past her daughter without even looking as the younger woman arranged napkins.

"There!" Karen cooed when all was ready, a gentle smile on her face as she looked over the beautifully laid table. Then she bellowed, "Boys! DINNER!"

Out of sight, Bailey's fingers tangled with the tablecloth as the sound of thundering feet drew closer.

The children arrived first, Will in the lead, with little Charlie dragging at his dressing gown.

"Oh, for God's sake, take those off," Monroe ordered, pulling the thick layers from her sons' shoulders. She turned an exasperated stare at the man who'd just stepped into the doorway. "Why did you put them in these? They'll get bloody heatstroke!"

"Not a pyjama day without dressing gowns," the man said

mildly. He was tall, like Monroe, but slight. His brown hair was thinning and his mouth was a touch too narrow; his grey shirt was wrinkled and his glasses were slightly wonky. But he had an endearingly distracted air about him that made his appearance charming, and somehow he managed to be handsome. His gaze came to rest on Bailey and he gave her a nod, his lips tilted in the ghost of a smile. "Hullo," he said. "George."

"Hi. I'm Bailey. Cash's friend."

"You're Uncle Cash's *girlfriend,*" giggled Charlie.

"He *likes* you," Will whispered, much more seriously. His small face was grave.

"Hey, now," Cash's voice came, playful and warm. "Don't give away all my secrets, boys." He walked into the room with his usual confidence, but there was something more there, after just a few hours at home—a kind of comfort, an inner contentedness that smoothed his sharp edges. He put his hand proprietorially on the back of Bailey's chair, then, after a moment's hesitation, bent down and kissed her forehead. The boys exploded into fits of laughter, and Bailey felt her cheeks heat.

"Quiet!" Monroe demanded. "Sit down. It's time to eat."

The chortles continued at a lower volume as the boys moved to the table, nudging each other hysterically. Monroe rolled her eyes and sat beside them, opposite Bailey. And then Bailey found herself between Cash on one side, and his mother on the other.

But by this point, she and Karen were practically best friends. Aside from Bailey's crippling fear of rejection and strong suspicion that no mother could ever truly accept her darling son's potential love interest, all was going swimmingly!

Or something.

"Help yourselves, help yourselves!" Karen cried, waving her hands expansively. "Dig in! George, what are you doing loitering by the window?"

George looked at the table with a faint expression of surprise. "Oh. Sorry, Karen." He wandered over to sit by his sons and began nibbling at a piece of garlic bread, his plate otherwise empty.

"Eat something, silly boy!" Karen demanded, piling her own plate with a small mountain of Bolognese.

"Daddy ate a whole box of After Eights," Charlie said around a string of spaghetti. "And he didn't let me have *any*."

"Bad for your teeth," George mumbled.

"Bad for *your* teeth," Monroe frowned. "Have some pasta."

"Leave me, Roe." But a smile played faintly about his lips

"Have some pasta," she said again, her voice firm.

He sighed dramatically, then reached for one of the huge serving dishes. Monroe rolled her eyes again, but she was clearly feigning exasperation, her cheeks pink and her smile slow. As if they were strangers flirting for the first time instead of bickering over dinner.

Bailey's eyes slid over to Cash. He winked at her, and she shovelled down a mouthful of Bolognese to stop herself from laughing.

"So!" Karen said. "*Bailey*. What a lovely name that is."

"Thanks," Bailey smiled. "It was my mother's maiden name."

"Really?" Karen let out a peal of laughter. "That's wonderful; you match my two! Last names as first names!"

"Oh, right," Bailey nodded. "Cash and Monroe. Yeah."

"Everyone thought I was a bit of an odd duck, with those names," Karen said, leaning in conspiratorially—as though the entire table and half the village couldn't hear her foghorn voice. "But I was being modern! Before my time, I was! Old is always new again, my love, you remember that."

"Where is your mother, Bailey?" George asked conversationally.

She looked up at him, startled by the question. "She passed away. A couple of years ago." Her gaze flew awkwardly to the kids, who were looking at her with twin expressions of fascination. Charlie's little mouth hung open, exposing a chewed up mound of Bolognese.

"Oh, I'm sorry. You have no family?"

"George," Monroe hissed, widening her eyes over the boys' heads.

"What?" he asked. "You told me to make conversation."

Monroe heaved out a sigh and let her head fall into her hands.

"Daddy," Will said helpfully, "I think you're doing the thing Mummy tells you not to do."

"Oh, dear," tutted Karen. "You must excuse our George. He's a bit funny."

"Mum!" Monroe cried.

"What, love? He is!" She turned to Bailey, patting her arm reassuringly. "He's very clever, you see. Clever people have nothing about them, everyone knows that."

Monroe groaned into her hands. Bailey tried very hard not to laugh. It didn't seem like the appropriate response.

"I'm just trying to find out why she's here," George said. "If she's not Cash's girlfriend, as he insists, then why has she come to take part in another family's Christmas? But of course, now that I know she is an orphan—"

"George, mate," Cash said. "Stop talking."

George shrugged and nibbled his garlic bread.

In the silence that followed, Bailey chewed her spaghetti and studied the room. Through the dining room window, she could see various Christmas lights flashing in the back garden. An illuminated Santa's grotto blinked red and white.

Suddenly, Cash set down his fork with a clatter. Bailey jumped and found his gaze drilling fiercely into her.

"Bailey is here because I want her to be," he said. "I invited her because she's important to me and because I wanted to spend Christmas with her." He reached out and grabbed her hand, holding it tight on top of the table. He was looking at his brother-in-law, but for some reason, she felt like he was talking to her. "Alright?"

George nodded as though nothing untoward had occurred. "Yep."

Then, as if on cue, the boys dissolved into fits of laughter again.

"Uncle Cash," Will wheezed between giggles. "You're holding hands with a *girl!*"

Cash gave Bailey a slow smile, the kind that felt like melted chocolate on her tongue. "Yep," he said.

Bailey aimed for a demure expression, one that showed she accepted all public admiration as her due. But she failed monumentally, and felt her face stretch into a goofy grin instead.

She could get used to this.

HOURS LATER, after dinner had been cleared up and the kids had been put to bed, Bailey found herself sitting in the living room with Monroe and a half-empty bottle of wine.

The room was vast, yet comfortable and homely. A fireplace sat at the far end, the mantelpiece covered by photographs and children's paintings. A wood fire burned merrily in the grate, the only source of light in the room aside from the tiny, winking bulbs adorning the Christmas tree.

And what a tree it was. The monstrous thing grazed the ceiling, with no room for a star or angel at its tip. Still, it was weighed down with crimson, gold and cream baubles, along with metres of tinsel and little plastic-wrapped candy canes. Underneath, a sea of beautifully-wrapped presents spread out on the carpet, eating into the room's space without remorse. It would take all bloody day to open those presents, Bailey thought, but she was more excited than annoyed at the prospect. Watching the kids open their gifts, and the adults, for that matter... It would be so different to the Christmases she and her mother had had, along with whichever man might be around at the time.

Not *better*, she told herself. Never that. But definitely something she'd always wanted to experience.

"You want more wine?" Monroe asked, and Bailey realised

with a start that the glass in her hand was empty. Oops.

"No, I should slow down."

"Rubbish. It's Christmas. Get wasted in the comfort of your own home."

Bailey chuckled, shaking her head. "I don't think so. Anyway, it's not my home. I'd hate to embarrass myself."

Monroe rolled her eyes. "Just you wait. Tomorrow's Christmas Eve; Mum will crack open the sherry and won't stop till Boxing Day. Then we'll see who's embarrassed."

They laughed together, and Bailey marvelled at how quickly the warm, open woman had started to feel like a friend.

But then Monroe's expression sobered. "Listen," she said, filling up her own glass. "About George—"

"Don't worry about it," Bailey said quickly. "Honestly. Don't."

"He really didn't mean any harm. He just doesn't think before he speaks. And he forgets that other people don't see things the way he does."

"Honestly, it's okay."

"He likes you, you know."

Bailey gave Monroe a blatantly sceptical look, and the other woman giggled.

"Okay, maybe I'm exaggerating. But he told me that you're 'both pretty and pleasant'." Her voice took on George's gentle, distant cadence.

"Oh, well. A ringing endorsement!"

"It's a hell of a lot better than his first comment on my character."

"Do I even want to know?"

Monroe shook her head with a snort. "Nope. You don't. Or you'll wonder why I married him."

Maybe, maybe not. Bailey had learned a long time ago that love was a tricky fucker.

As though she'd spoken the thought aloud, Monroe murmured, "My brother really *does* like you, though. Doesn't he?"

"Oh, I don't know. I suppose so."

"You suppose so? I've never heard him talk about a woman like that. Not ever. Certainly not in front of everyone!"

Bailey shifted awkwardly on the sofa, tucking her feet under her bum. She wasn't entirely sure how to respond to that. She wasn't entirely sure about anything when it came to Cash and their 90-day sex fest that wasn't even a sex fest yet. But she did know that his words at dinner had lit a spark in her—not one that burned comet-bright and faded just as fast, or one that seared away her good sense. No; it glowed gently, warming her up from the inside out. It didn't feel like a dangerous love. It felt like the kind of secret that was a pleasure to keep.

Monroe was watching her closely. In the low light, the woman's blue eyes looked eerily like Cash's green ones. "My brother is a complicated man," she said. "We had some difficult times growing up."

Bailey nodded. She'd heard as much from Cash himself. But then Monroe's next words caught her completely by surprise.

"Our father beat the shit out of Mum."

Bailey's mouth opened, but nothing came out. What the hell did you say to that?

"He was a monster. He was obsessed with her. There was nowhere for her to hide. She ran away and took us with her, and it worked for a while. But in the end, he'd find us, and he'd punish her." Monroe swirled her wine around the glass, as though they were discussing nothing heavier than tomorrow's menu. "So I suppose we're all a little bit fucked. Which is fine. But Cash—"

"What about me?"

Bailey jumped at the sudden sound of his voice, her heart stuttering. In the shadows of the hallway, Cash leant against the doorframe. Darkness danced with light across the sardonic twist of his mouth. His hair fell forward, hiding his eyes almost completely, but she could still see that glint of green, like a tiger peering through tall grass.

Fuck.

CHAPTER 19

Monroe leaned back against the sofa cushions, her expression resigned. “Hello, little brother.”

“Hello, Roe. Spinning fairytales again?”

“Fairytales?” Her voice was sharp, defiant.

“Turning me into a tortured hero?” He stepped into the room, his arms folded, his jaw set. “Don’t bother. It stretches the limits of imagination too far.”

Monroe stood up. “Don’t—”

But Bailey could see what Monroe apparently couldn’t. Cash was on the edge of absolute fury; every inch of him was vibrating, the lines of his face terrible in their severity. And the last thing anyone needed was a God-awful war the night before Christmas Eve.

So she leapt up and went to him, pressing her hand against his chest. Forcing him to concentrate on something other than the demons chasing his shadow.

“I’m tired,” she said. Then, when he continued to stare over her head, his face iron: “*Cash*. I’m tired. I want to go to bed.”

He looked down at her, finally, his eyes focusing on her face. His expression softened, just a bit. “Alright,” he said. “Come on, then. Let’s go.”

He turned on his heel and left the room without looking back. Bailey followed, throwing Monroe an apologetic glance over her shoulder. She was rewarded with a wry smile and a shake of the head.

Crisis averted. Maybe.

Cash led her through the now-dark halls and up two flights of stairs. "We're on the top floor," he explained, the strain easing from his voice with every step. "Mum chose rooms for us all when we got the house. She wanted me to have skylights."

"Who else is up here?" she whispered in the darkness, staying close to him, tracing his path by the moonlight beaming through the hallway windows. He passed one door and stopped at the next.

"Right now? No-one. Just us. So you don't need to whisper." He pushed the door open and flicked on the light, then took her hand and pulled her into the room.

His mother might have chosen it for him, but she'd decorated it generically. Like the rest of the house, it was done in warm, neutral tones with flashes of colour here and there; in this case, sky blue. Still, it was big and warm, and the soft, cream carpet was heavenly beneath Bailey's feet.

There was a bed. A large bed. But just the one.

Obviously.

She turned to face Cash, suddenly hesitant. "Did you put my things in here?"

"Yeah," he said softly. "Is that okay?"

"Um… Yes. Of course. I mean, this is fine." She sounded like she was convincing herself more than him, and she knew it. He smiled, the expression chasing away the last of the tension on his face. Which made her embarrassment worth it.

He held her hands tightly, his thumb tracing over her knuckles.

"Bailey," he murmured, almost to himself. His smile faded, replaced by something painfully tender. He pulled her forward, inch by inch, until the only thing between them was the covenant of their joined hands. Then he lowered his head, pressed his cheek to hers, and whispered in her ear. "You are divine. You're like sunlight through stained glass. This isn't how I thought things would be." He kissed the hollow just behind her earlobe, and she gasped, her head spinning.

His lips moved lower, grazing along the line of her throat, and blooming desire became urgent need. "How—how did you think it would be?" she whispered.

"Heavy. Thick as blood. Not like this. Not like breathing. And I love it." He pressed his face to her skin, inhaled. "I knew I would, but… You feel like satisfaction. Like every summer I ever had. Should I be worried?"

She was asking herself the same question. But she pressed her palms against his chest and felt his heart beating like a hummingbird's wings, and she said, "Trust me."

He pulled away, looking into her eyes as though they held the secrets of the world. "I do," he said. "I do trust you. I don't trust me."

This was the part where she asked him why. Where she cast light over every shadow that had ever passed through his gemstone eyes. But he'd told her what he wanted, and it wasn't questions and intimacy and—and whatever it was that made her blossom beneath his touch. Cash wanted one thing from her, and it was something she knew how to give. So she rose up onto her toes and pressed her body against his and kissed him.

Kissing him was just like being kissed by him, only better, because a man wanting her was nothing special, but Bailey wanting a man, wanting him and chasing him—that was impossible. Impossible was Cash.

She pulled at the fabric of his T-shirt, letting her desperation out of its cage, letting her need see the moonlight, even if it could never walk in the sun. And Cash crumbled just for her, wrapping his arms around her as though they were lost at sea, drinking down her kisses like they were life itself. His hands went to her hips, as they always seemed to, and she allowed herself to acknowledge the way *he* wanted—wanted desperately, wanted her, Bailey, before he wanted any woman—because his hands told her so; the way they grabbed, so hungry, so lustful, told her so. Her, and him. No-one else. It couldn't be anyone else.

He walked her back towards the bed and pushed her down before she realised she was falling. The mattress hugged her like heaven, let her bounce back up, and then he came too and weighed her down, earthing the current that flowed through her veins.

"Clothes off," he told her. "I always see you naked, when I dream of you. Clothes off."

"And you?"

"Whatever you want," he said, rising up on his knees.

"Good." She sat and pulled her jumper up over her head. Heat flared in his eyes as she leant back on her hands, her chest bare. He moved to touch her, but she pulled away.

"You, too, remember? You said whatever I want."

He laughed and stood and stripped. His T-shirt flew and the full extent of his sleeve was revealed: the ink wrapped around his shoulder, fading into a winged chest piece. Then he unbuttoned his jeans, shoving them off along with his briefs, and straightened before her. She didn't know where to look first; at the ink curling over his hips; at the muscle cording his thighs; at the thick, straining column of his erection.

Wait. Yes, she did.

She surged forward and reached for him, but he stepped back, his face tight with desire.

"Keep going," he said, nodding at her clothes.

And so she stood too, and pulled off her long skirt, and thanked God she wasn't wearing her awful, tight jeans, and that her healing tattoo was no longer a sticky mess.

He dragged his gaze over her body, from head to toe, and she basked in his lust, letting it warm her through.

"You're not naked yet," he said softly.

She reached up and pulled off her glasses, her smile teasing.

He took them from her with a smirk, putting them on the drawers by the door.

"Nice try, Bailey. Keep going."

She looked down and—oops. There he stood like a fucking god, like the image of sex itself, and here she was in her *Beauty and the Beast* knickers. Not an easy situation to take control of. But she rather thought she could regain the upper hand.

With a smirk of her own, Bailey turned slowly, presenting her back to him. Her back, and something he'd always liked far better.

Bending over, she tucked her fingers into the waistband of her underwear and slid them slowly down, over the curve of her arse. He released a low groan as they made their way down her thighs.

"Fuck," he rasped. She felt his hands on her, a palm gripping each cheek as he explored the expanse of round flesh. She stepped out of her underwear a moment before he spread her wide, pushing her further forwards. And then, suddenly, his warm breath skated across her slick, exposed folds.

She braced herself against the bed, opening her legs wider, bending lower, pushing wantonly back towards his mouth. And he obliged her silent request, his hot tongue sliding along her slit in a move that made her ache, right down to her bones. His tongue toyed with her clit until she felt dizzy.

"I owe you," he said, pulling back, and his voice was thick and smoky. "I owe you five orgasms at least."

"But you didn't finish when I…"

"Doesn't matter. Five minutes of heaven equals five orgasms." He eased two thick fingers inside her, stroking the sensitive walls of her pussy with a confidence that seemed almost obscene. She moaned, and he laughed darkly, his exhalations caressing her skin. "I think we can manage it. Don't you?"

"I… Um… Oh!" Bailey's word broke off in a little shriek as the tip of his tongue swept over her swollen clit. "*Fuck*, do that again."

He did, and then again, faster, and faster—all the while

plunging his fingers into her cunt until her back bowed and her breath left her body. Bailey cried out her desperation as he pushed her closer to climax, his thick fingers and clever tongue claiming her in a sensual assault. His tongue strayed for a moment to join his fingers at her entrance, lapping at her growing wetness, and he moaned as he tasted her. His licks grew frantic, as though he couldn't get enough of the molten desire dripping from her pussy—but then, finally, he returned to torturing her swollen clit. She felt his soft lips on her and shivered. He sucked. She broke. Writhing against the blankets, Bailey came with a shudder and a low, guttural sigh.

He pushed her forward until she was lying fully on the bed, left limp as a doll by pleasure. Then he followed, lying on his side next to her her, and she rolled onto her back. His hair hung down as he looked at her, studying her face as though committing the features to memory. She smiled hazily and reached up to play with the silken strands.

"There," he whispered. "That's just how you look at me when I dream of us."

"Do you do that often?" she asked, teasing.

He traced a finger across her lips, following the curve of her smile—but his own face was serious. "Yes," he murmured. "I do."

CASH KNEW that he was saying too much. He knew that even if he could keep his mouth shut—if he could choke down the adoration that sprang from his chest like wildflowers—his body would give him away. Because surely she must know, when he touched her like this, that he needed her.

And yet, she wasn't afraid of his intensity. She wasn't running. She looked up at him with trust in her eyes—trust, and something softer. Something harder to spot and infinitely more precious. Something so bright, he was forced to look away from its brilliance. Her fingers twisted his hair gently, playfully. Her legs, smooth and soft and plump, tangled up with his. And she still wanted him.

He leaned down and kissed her, let his feelings pour out in silence through the medium of lips and tongue. She pulled him closer and mewled like a kitten and arched into him so trustingly that he forgot himself completely. He settled over her, hooking an arm under her leg and pushing it up out of his way. Then he shifted forwards until the head of his aching cock came to rest against the heaven that was her cunt. But the minute that searing heat pressed against him, he let out a defeated sigh.

"Fuck. Condom."

She huffed, pouted, and he laughed.

"What's up, kitten?"

"If you're gonna get me all worked up—"

"All worked up, hm?" He climbed off the bed and stood up, taking a moment to admire her laid out before him like an unwrapped gift. The flare of her hips, the dark velvet of her skin, her hair splayed out like ribbons around her head. Then he forced himself to cross the room, snatching protection from his luggage. Opening the box as he walked, Cash returned to the bed, pulling out a condom and tossing the rest aside. He tore it open and sheathed himself with the ease of practice, then climbed over Bailey, settling between her legs like the space was made for him.

But then she traced her fingers over the ink on his ribs, and he stiffened. Held his breath. Waited.

"You have a scar," she murmured, stroking the thick ridge of tissue that he'd half- hidden with pitch-black ink. But of all the women he'd ever been with, of course she'd be the one to notice. The one who truly saw him, whether he wanted it or not.

"Yeah," he managed.

"How—?"

He bent down and kissed her, soft and teasing. By the time he pulled back, she was silent, a smile curving her lips. But still, she touched the scar. So he kissed her again, his tongue sliding against hers until she moaned into his mouth and writhed beneath him. Until his heart stopped racing and his skin stopped prickling and the lazy, liquid heat of desire overtook the sharp bite of panic in his gut.

She stared up at him, her eyes wide, her lips parted, and he prayed he'd see her just like this a hundred thousand times before he died. Then she put her fingertips to his cheek and wrapped her legs around his waist and said, "Cash. Need you now." And every thought but one left his head.

He positioned himself at her entrance, felt her wet heat calling to him. Thrust forward, slow and steady, his rock-hard cock pushing its way into her tight cunt as she fluttered around him.

"Fuck," she gasped, sinking into the satisfaction. He wondered if she felt as divine, being filled, as he felt filling her. "Fuck, fuck, *fuck—*"

He kissed her, swallowed her need as she set his every nerve-ending on fire. When he settled himself to the hilt in her sweet, soft pussy, she moaned against his lips, and he thought he'd lose it in that very moment.

But he didn't. He held on. Eased back from the death-grip of her cunt, the friction so delicious it sent sparks flying behind his eyes. Thrust deep, again and again. She gasped in his ear, pressed her sweat-slick body to his, panting and swearing and raking her nails across his back. Every desperate command she gave made his balls tighten, but he ignored her, shook his head when she told him *faster*. Kept his pace steady. Stoked the flames higher and higher, until Bailey looked like she might faint with pleasure.

"Please," she whimpered, clutching his biceps. "I'm so fucking close."

"I did promise you five, didn't I?" he panted, grinding into her, still achingly slow despite his words. "I bet you're so pretty when you come."

"Faster," she begged. "God, you fuck me so good."

"Bailey," he groaned, his control slipping. "You feel amazing. How will it feel when you come on my cock?" He was finally giving her what she wanted—what *he* needed. He opened her legs wider, bringing them up to rest against his shoulders as he moved faster and faster. Then he reached between their bodies and rubbed her clit in rough, firm circles. Her pussy tightened around him, milking him, sending raw heat roaring through his veins. When he bent his head to suck the stiff peak of her nipple, she came again, just like that.

She was fucked, because from that point on, he had her number. Over and over again he drove her to the edge, grinning even as he panted from exertion, murmuring dirty, filthy praise even as he clawed for his own restraint. He pumped into her, stroked that swollen pearl between her legs, kneaded her sweet little breasts, and she whimpered and bit her own fist and broke into pieces for him every time.

"I'm sorry," he grunted when his rhythm finally stuttered, as his thrusts became frantic and his body burned with passion. "Four will have to do. You're too fucking—"

"What?" Bailey grinned now, lifting her hips. "I'm too what?"

"Perfect," he rasped. And then, finally, after teetering endlessly at the precipice, Cash followed her over the edge.

CHAPTER 20

Cash had the best sleep of his life in Bailey's arms. When he awoke the next morning, he found the room bathed in a pale light that reflected his mood perfectly. Peace reigned, from the winter sun streaming in through the windows to the light tapping of computer keys coming from the chair in the corner of the room.

Until the tapping turned faster, sharper, more irritable. He opened his eyes just as taps turned to slaps. Bailey was curled up in the armchair, smacking at her laptop, frustration all over her face.

"What's up?" Cash frowned. She looked up at him, and he was alarmed to see tears gleaming in her dark eyes.

"My laptop's fucked. And I think I just lost the last two thousand words of my dissertation."

"Shit." He got up out of bed, barely noticing the fact that he was still naked. The two of them had stayed up late into the night, exploring each other's bodies in both desire and innocence, running through the box of condoms like they were going out of style. He'd been hoping for more of the same this morning, but clearly that wasn't going to happen. Bailey looked ready to throw something or burst into tears, and neither of those options sounded good to him.

"Hey," he soothed, kneeling before her and pulling the clunky old laptop from her hands. "Don't worry. You have plenty of time, right? Your deadline's not for months."

She sniffed. "How do you know that?"

"I do listen when you talk, you know."

"I never told you that," she insisted.

He winced. "Yeah. I listen when you talk, but you're not always talking to me."

At least that admission, embarrassing as it was, shocked the misery off of her face. She giggled slightly, pressing her hand to his cheek, and he let himself lean into the touch. She was wearing one of his T-shirts, and, he suspected, a pair of his boxers. Despite himself, he felt his cock harden.

She looked down and arched a brow. "Seriously?"

"What?"

"Aren't you tired?"

He waggled his eyebrows. "Are you?"

"Stop," she laughed. But then her expression sobered. "Fuck. I don't know what I'm gonna do about my laptop."

"Ah," he said. "Right. Well, I wouldn't worry about that too much."

"How can I not?!" She shook her head frantically, dislodging her glasses. He pushed them safely back up her nose and was rewarded with a glare.

"Hang on," he sighed, getting up. While she grumbled under her breath, he went over to the wardrobe, where he'd dumped their luggage last night. He unzipped his suitcase—yes, he'd brought a suitcase, but in his defence, it was 80% presents—and pulled out the biggest box. Just like the rest, it was wrapped in brown paper that he'd picked up from the post office. But this one had a red ribbon around it, tied in as close an approximation of a bow as he could manage.

He returned to Bailey's little corner of the room, putting the box in her lap. "Here you go," he said. "Merry Christmas."

She pursed her lips. "It's Christmas Eve."

"Merry early Christmas."

"What is it?"

"Open it and found out."

She winced. "It's not expensive, is it?"

"Come on, woman. Open the bloody present."

"It's not a laptop, is it? Please tell me it's not a laptop."

"It's not a laptop," he said. She gave him a hard look, then cracked a smile and pulled off the ribbon, tearing into the paper with barely-disguised glee.

"Oh, my God. Cash! You said it wasn't a laptop!" He watched as Bailey gaped at the box in her lap, smoothing her fingers over the picture on the front.

"It's not," he said smugly. "It's a MacBook."

"A MacBook is a laptop."

"Nope. A MacBook is a MacBook."

She smacked the back of his head lightly. "Stop that. I can't accept—"

"What you *can't* do is reject a Christmas present, you ungrateful wench."

"But—"

"Bailey. Come on. You said it yourself; you need something to work on. And I don't want you using a piece of crap that loses your work. Although," he added with a grin, "that's really your own fault. You should save it to a memory stick every few hundred words."

"You're insufferable," she huffed, rolling her eyes. But her fingers curled around the edges of the box, and she looked down at it with a mixture of awe and pleasure. "I just… This is really thoughtful of you, Cash." She laughed suddenly. "The present I got you is kind of terrible in comparison."

"Impossible," he said, standing up. "If it's from you, I'm sure it'll be perfect."

"That's a very sweet thing to say." She squinted up at him mockingly. "Actually, are you feeling okay? You're being unbelievably pleasant this morning."

"Yep. Cuz I finally got you into bed." He grabbed her hand and pulled her up into his arms. Then he reached around her and squeezed her arse hungrily. "You should come back and top me up before the effects wear off."

She tutted, rolling her eyes at him. But she followed him willingly as he walked backwards to the bed, their bodies tangling together. And she kissed him happily as he pulled down the boxers she was wearing. And she moaned for him five minutes later.

So he guessed she didn't really mind.

"Will!" Monroe hollered. "Play nicely! Are you listening to me?"

Will took the toy car off of his little brother's head with a guilty pout. "Yes, Mum."

"I don't know why you cluck over them, sweetheart," said Karen. "When you and your brother were little you'd stuff rocks up his nose and all sorts."

Monroe gave her mother a horrified look. Cash shared an amused glance with Bailey, who was sitting on the carpet with the kids, but doing little to temper the… *enthusiasm* of their play. Turned out she was a total pushover. George, who was tapping away at both a laptop and a tablet at once, grunted something that might have been a laugh.

As the sun sank into the trees, the living room became a breathing embodiment of Christmas Eve. They'd spent the day playing hide and seek in the huge, icy garden—which George was especially good at—and then Mum and Bailey had done some baking with the boys after lunch. Now every belly was full, yet homemade gingerbread remained piled on the coffee table. The TV was on, playing a *Shrek* film that the boys had insisted be recorded—but of course, they weren't watching it at all. The fire crackled, the kids bickered, as did Cash's mother and sister.

And his woman sat there in the middle of it all, exactly where he wanted her.

She caught him staring, gave him a shy smile. "What?" she asked, pushing her glasses up her nose.

"You look beautiful," he told her, his voice low.

Her smile widened, and she looked down, letting her hair swing over her face. He liked that. He liked making her shy, and he liked making her smile.

So fucking much.

"I'm very pleased for you, Cash," George said suddenly.

"You are?" Cash grinned at his baffling brother-in-law, though the man hadn't looked up from his glowing computer screens. "Why's that?"

"Roe has always been worried that you would close yourself off completely. But now you're in love, like us."

Cash stared. His mouth became dry, and sound filtered into his ears as though through a tunnel. The kids, the TV, whatever his sister was currently saying to George—it all faded into the background. And all he saw was Bailey's shocked face, as though he'd zoomed in on her like a picture on a screen.

Then, all at once, every sense returned, slapping him in the face with their intensity. Just in time for him to hear himself say far too vehemently: "I'm not in love with Bailey."

Silence fell. Actual silence. It was broken only by the sound of Shrek grousing at Donkey on the TV. Funny, really; irreverence was the backing track to what felt like the heaviest moment of his life.

Bailey looked like she'd been slapped. All the warmth fled her skin, as though the blood had drained from her face.

Cash stood, panic descending like a mist.

"Really?" George asked, clearly confused. "Because I was quite sure—"

"Shut up," Monroe muttered. Then she stood too and clapped

her hands. "Time for bed, boys!" she trilled, her voice reaching a decibel that would do their mother proud.

Oh, fuck. Mum. She was right there, staring at him with disappointment in her eyes.

And what the fuck was he supposed to do with that? Disappointment for what? He'd done everything right, everything he could to avoid turning out like the monster who'd fathered him. He wasn't going to risk it all now, just for a woman whose touch was pure sunlight. He was stronger than that. This was strength.

"But it's not even late!" Will was moaning.

"Do as your mother says," George told him. As though everything was fine. As though Cash's world wasn't splintering.

"I'm not in love with Bailey," he said again, insistent.

Monroe turned to glare at him. "I think we heard you the first time!" she snapped.

But he barely noticed her. He focused on Bailey's face, on the tears threatening to spill over her lashes. And he saw the exact moment when she reigned them in, when she set her jaw and straightened her spine and locked him out of her heart forever.

And he had no idea why the sight felt like a death.

He looked to the right, where his mother remained—for once in her life—stonily silent, and then to the left where George —*fucking* George—continued to frown at him sceptically. And panic continued to claw at his throat, drawing blood.

"I… I have to go," he choked out. He pushed past his sister and his nephews on their way out of the living room, stumbling into the hall. He had enough presence of mind to shove on his boots and grab a coat. Then he unlocked the front door and stepped out into the icy evening.

CHAPTER 21

Bailey shoved her ancient laptop into her holdall with shaking hands. It took three tries, but she finally forced the wide, plastic carcass past the zipper of the bag. Her breaths were rapid, laboured, as if she'd just run a mile—but she hadn't run at all. No; she'd left the living room and climbed each flight of stairs at a sedate pace, as though she were a duchess and not an interloper who'd just been quite firmly put in her place.

Shit.

Releasing a long, shaking sigh, she sat down heavily on the bed. The bed where just last night, she'd allowed herself to believe that she'd found an impossible man. A man who was capable of real partnership.

Of real love.

She should never have judged her mother. But Bailey hadn't realised just how convincing men could be. How they could speak with a look, with a touch, and then open their mouths and bring the fantasy crashing down.

Fuck, Cash had been clear from the start. He'd told her exactly what he wanted. She'd agreed! And still, she ended up ascribing impossible values to intangible things. Ended up developing *feelings,* for Christ's sake. She'd made a damned fool of herself, and she deserved the humiliation of his obvious disgust.

But she didn't have to like it.

With a huff, Bailey tore off her glasses, swiping angrily at the tears that threatened to overflow from her lashes. Ridiculous. Was she a child to tantrum over rejection, and from a man she barely knew? Her own mother had handled divorces with more dignity than this.

Clutching that thought tightly to her heart, Bailey took a deep breath. Then another, and another, until the shard of ice in her chest felt like nothing more than a splinter. She cleaned her glasses on the bed sheet and pushed them back into place, then tied her locs up neatly.

There. Now she was being sensible. Now she was in control.

First things first: she had no ride. If she wanted to leave, that meant ordering a taxi to the middle of nowhere on Christmas Eve. And she was pretty sure that Uber wouldn't be an option.

Okay, so she'd Google it. The price would be astronomical, but she had some savings. Humiliated flight from her boss's family home wasn't exactly what she'd intended to use those savings for, but whatever.

Her movements calmer now, she stood and went over to the little pile of luggage Cash had left by the wardrobe. Between their busy night and a day spent entertaining the kids, they hadn't really had time to unpack. Her mother would've called that a sign.

Some of their things had been pulled out and left on top of the pile, though, and Bailey spied one of her favourite cardigans amongst the mess. She wasn't about to leave that behind, or anything else; if he had to return any of her things at work, she'd die of mortification.

God, work. She'd have to see him every day. Everyone would want to know how their Christmas went. Of course, that was assuming he wouldn't sack her, after this mess. But he'd never do something like that.

Would he?

Bailey flicked through her mental Rolodex of men, the archetypes she'd created through years of watching her mother's mistakes. For what felt like the thousandth time, she tried to figure out exactly what kind of man Cash Evans really was.

There was The Roger: a guy who was looking for a trophy, a badge of honour, another enviable possession for his collection.

That wasn't Cash. If it was, he'd hardly go for a girl like her.

Okay. The Paul: a mess of a man whose big dreams were eclipsed only by his sense of entitlement. Work was for others; rewards were his due. Probably called his bedmates *Mummy*. Thought 'girlfriend' was code for 'live-in maid' and 'wife' was code for 'slave'.

But Cash didn't fit that mould either.

Who else?

The Mike: desperate to be loved—not to love in return, but to feel like he was worth something. Charming one minute, hateful the next. Every insult he sent your way was originally meant for himself. Toxic to the core. Wanted a punching bag with a pussy.

Was that Cash? The man who'd spent all day playing tirelessly with his nephews, the man who worshipped his mother in his own quiet way and loved his sister so dearly?

She was starting to think that he didn't fit into any of her categories. In fact, the more she considered the man she'd come to know, the more she thought that he might simply be... *good.*

Good, and not at all in love with her. Outright opposed to the idea, in fact. Obviously.

Irritated, Bailey tugged roughly at the sleeve of one of her cardigans, hanging out from beneath all their other luggage. It came loose—and pulled down the whole pile of stuff with it. For fuck's sake.

She knelt on the floor and picked everything up. It was mostly Cash's: his clothes, the box of condoms they'd almost emptied. She felt her cheeks heat up and hated herself for it. And—what was this?

A sketchbook. Not the kind she'd seen before, the kind he left lying around the shop and bought in bulk because he went through them so fast. This one was smaller, heavier, bound in buttery leather. A loose sheaf of pages hung from its edge—they must have been dislodged when everything fell. Bailey picked up the book with brisk hands, pushing the loose pages back in.

But then her gaze caught on a slice of familiarity, cast in black Biro. The corner of a smile, the edge of a thick pair of glasses, a few long locs.

That was her. Cash had drawn her.

She eased the paper slowly out from the sketchbook's embrace, her heart pounding. She shouldn't be doing this. It felt like reading somebody's diary. A small part of her brain said *Fuck him, anyway!* But most of her was horrified at her own audacity. Not to mention her weakness. She shouldn't want to look inside his head—she shouldn't even want to look at *him.*

The page slid free and she came face to face with herself, and her doubts disappeared. She simply didn't have room for them anymore.

God, he was talented. She hadn't known that he could do this—portraiture, and so realistic, too. The drawing took up the whole page; just her, smiling at nothing, wearing one of her Christmas jumpers, the one with the snowflake pattern. The image was cut off just below her chest, but that was enough to recognise her clothing. In the corner, he'd written: *Bailey, life, 16/12/17.*

She turned the page over. There was more.

This side featured multiple drawings, much smaller than the other one, and more cartoon-like in style. There were four, and she was in all of them. But she wasn't always alone.

In the first, she was drawn from above, lying down in bed. Naked. She remembered his words the night before: *I always see you naked, when I dream of you.* Her locs were arranged into heart-shapes that fanned out around her head, scattered with roses.

The sight made her smile. Then she wiped her expression clean. No smiling. No softening. No weakness.

In the second ,she was another version of herself, a winged version whose hair rose about her head in a maelstrom, with terrible eyes and a wicked smile, wearing a gown that looked like a dark wedding dress.

In the third, she was her usual self, clad in jeans and a jumper, but she held hands with someone whose body was just out of frame. Only their forearm was visible. A forearm decorated in familiar ink, tentacles wrapping around its wrist.

In the fourth, she was sitting cross-legged on the floor. There was a smiling, curly-haired toddler in her lap.

She stared at the fourth picture for a long time. A long, long time.

Then she opened the sketchbook.

Bailey, life, 21/12/17. Bailey, 17/12/17. Bailey, life, 12/12/17. She worked back from the middle to the front

09/12/17.

28/11/17.

20/11/17.

Bailey, life, 30/10/17.

What the fuck? In these images, she was in the coffee shop, her sleeves rolled up and her hair in a bun, steaming milk or stacking mugs or serving a customer.

He'd been drawing her since the coffee shop?

She flicked to the very first page. It was a quick sketch of she and Tara, laughing together behind the counter. Labelled *Coffee Girl, life, 12/10/2017.* In bold, block caps beneath the label, Cash had written: TOMORROW, FIND OUT HER NAME.

She remembered that day. The first time he'd come in, dragged by a pretty girl with blue hair and a lip ring. She'd never seen the girl again.

But she'd seen Cash.

A light knock interrupted her snooping. She dropped the

book like it was on fire, then picked it up again and closed it carefully, laying it on top of Cash's suitcase.

"Hello?" she called, rising awkwardly. Her left foot had gone to sleep.

"It's me, love!" came the loud response.

Biting her lip, Bailey sat down on the bed. "Come in."

The door swung open and Karen entered like a tornado, crossing the room in what felt like a single swoop. She pulled Bailey up off the bed and into her arms, her ample cleavage like a pillow to the gut.

"Oh, you poor thing. That bloody son of mine. Ooooh, I could throttle him!" Her grip on Bailey came dangerously close to a similar level of violence. But she let go suddenly and stepped back, slapping her palms to her cheeks. She looked like a cartoon character. "Monroe told me not to get involved. I told her bugger off, it's my right to get involved; and anyway, I'm not getting involved! I just wanted to tell you something—"

"Karen," Bailey said. "You really don't need to—"

But the other woman interrupted Bailey with a wail, her gaze going to the holdall on the bed. "Oh, Lord, you're packing! You're not going, are you? How will you get home? Well, of course, George would drive you. But I don't want you to leave! That won't do at all. Cash can leave! It would serve him right! He lives to give me grey hairs, that boy." She shook her head. "Listen, now Bailey, I know I've got a cheek. But I like you. I really do. And I like what you've done for my boy."

"I haven't done anything for him," Bailey mumbled.

"Oh, now *that's* not true." Karen plopped herself down on the bed and patted the space beside her, waiting until Bailey sank reluctantly onto the mattress. "He rings me every day, you know. But I suppose he never told you that."

Bailey's brows shot up in surprise. "...No, he never..."

"Doesn't fit his *image,* I'm sure. You know these magazines and all, they think he's a proper bad boy! Honestly. My little Cashew Nut! Well." Karen adjusted her apron with a sniff. Lord only knew why she was still wearing the thing, but she rarely seemed to take it off. "It started when he went on his little world tour. He was very anxious about leaving me to my own devices, so he called me at least once a day. But never mind that; I'm waffling. I only came up to say one thing, just one thing! Is that alright?"

Karen was gazing at Bailey very seriously, as though it really would take just a word for her to leave without completing her speech. But the little woman was near bursting with desperation; that much was obvious.

"Okay," Bailey said. Her voice was almost a whisper.

"Good. Good. Well. Now I barely know where to begin! But I should tell you the whole story, shouldn't I? So: I met Cash's father when I was fifteen. He was twenty-seven years old."

CHAPTER 22

Bailey blinked as her mind struggled to absorb that information. But Karen was still going, her voice unusually high and tight, her gaze focused on the carpet.

"His name was Henry. He was the caretaker at my school. There was a group of girls that used to pick on me, but when Henry saw them, he'd always run them off. He... he was my hero, back then.

"So when I was sixteen, we ran off to Gretna Green. My dad was absolutely furious. He never spoke to me again. And Henry, he got in all sorts of trouble with the school—they sacked him. So we moved away. That's when the problems started."

Bailey's fingers pulled at the bedsheets, tightening around the fabric as she prepared for the next part of Karen's history. She knew enough of monstrous men to see where this was going.

"I lost touch with all my friends from school, of course. Henry struggled to get another job. He started to believe that I was a bad luck charm, that I was ruining his life. He said I'd bewitched him and forced him to disgrace himself and now he was stuck with me. He—he would beat me and beg me to let him go. I thought that he was right. I thought I must be tying him to me somehow, forcing him to hurt me, and I just wasn't clever enough to stop it."

Karen's voice had gone from frenetic to wooden, utterly dead. She relayed the terrible history with no emotion whatsoever, as if she had left her body and the words emitting from her mouth were simply a robotic recording.

The two women were sitting side by side, but Karen might as well have been a distant star. She was alone, apart, lifetimes away, as she continued. "When I fell pregnant, I thought that it would help. And it did, for a little while—until Monroe came out a girl. He hadn't wanted that. It was my fault, of course—it always was. Another useless witch, he said, just like me. He was happier when Cash came along, but eventually, he went back to his old ways. I tried to hide it from the children, but I know that I failed. They were with me every second of the day. Makeup and a smile never worked on them.

"I thought about leaving—I thought about it all the time, but I had nowhere to go. I wrote to my parents, and my mother wrote back to say... to say that Dad was dead." Karen's voice cracked as she held back a sob. "And I wasn't welcome. She didn't want any of my trouble. I thought about going to the police, but I thought, what will that achieve? Henry might get a slap on the wrist. A social worker would come and they'd put my kids on some bloody list. Next thing you know, I'm an unfit mother and they're in care." She gave a shrill, humourless laugh and muttered, "Over my dead body."

Karen was panting now, her face twisted with pain, but she soldiered on—as though she couldn't pause, couldn't take even a second, or she might never continue. "So I waited. I was biding my time, doing my best to shield the kids—but it didn't work. As Cash got older... God, you see the size of him. He was taller than me by the time he was nine. And he started to fight back. Trying to protect me, though I told him not to. Henry laughed it off at first; knocked him aside, hit him a time or two, to put him in his place. But Cash just got bigger and angrier. When he was twelve, he came into my room and found me crying. I tried to hide my face from him, but he pulled my hands away, and he saw what

Henry had done, and I thought he would explode. He went running down the stairs and he dragged Henry out of his chair and threw him to the floor. And that was the day Henry began to see his son as a threat.

"They fought. Cash lost. He was beaten bloody. Monroe was hysterical, I was hysterical. Henry was smug. He told me I'd spoilt the boy, but it would all end now. And the look on his face when he said that—he was excited." Karen's voice caught, but after a ragged pause she continued. "He went out to the pub, and I knew he would come home drunk. I had to act fast. I'd been saving up, stealing from Henry—he hated giving me money, and I had none of my own, but Monroe is clever with numbers. She always knew what to do. We'd take a little from the shopping budget here and there, and he'd never even notice.

"We had eighty-three pounds and fifty-two pence. We kept it in a silver purse Monroe had, a child's thing. And we ran. Cash was a mess; two of his teeth were knocked out. His right hand was so swollen and bloody he could barely move it. We hurried down the street in the dark, and he kept whispering—*Mum, what if I can't draw anymore?"* She let out a choked little laugh. "That boy." And despite herself, despite her horror, Bailey felt herself smiling tearily at the thought of a young Cash in dire circumstances, worrying about his art.

"We took the bus across five counties," Karen said. "It wasn't like today; there were no mobile phones or internet apps. We didn't know where to go. We wound up in some dingy little city and it took us two days to find a shelter. One of those feminist places. It was lovely." A dreamy smile took over her face. But then, just as quickly, it faded. "And it was less than two months before he found us. Henry."

Fuck. There was more? Hearing this was like listening in on a horror story. Knowing that it had actually happened, that it wasn't simply a story? Bailey thought her heart would break.

"The woman who managed the shelter—tough as old boots, she was. She held him off at the door. I remember her voice now.

She told him, 'Fuck off, pal. You ain't coming in here.' And he blustered and swore but she just laughed in his face. I-I couldn't believe it. He threatened her, and she said... she said, 'My doorway is a line. You cross it, and you'll find my boot up your backside.' And he... he left! He just left!

"But we couldn't stay. There were other women in the shelter, other children, and I knew he would come back. The manager gave me some money before I went, out of her own pocket, bless her. That money saved us more than once. There's a lot of kindness in this world, you know, hiding beneath the evil."

Bailey wanted, more than anything, to hold Karen's hand. To remind her that they were living in the present, that she was safe now. But then Bailey realised: she had no idea if Karen was safe. She had no idea how this story ended.

"We kept moving, never settling at first. He chased us. We had nowhere to go, no-one to help us—it was so awful. I can't even tell you. A lot of that time seems like a story I heard, a nightmare that someone else experienced. But Monroe has no GCSEs and Cash has precious few. When I remember that, I remember everything. And I remember that it's my fault." A sob tore through her, shaking her body. Bailey bit her lip and finally gave in to the urge to offer comfort. Without a word, she put her arm around Karen's narrow shoulders. And though the older woman said nothing, didn't even look at Bailey, she didn't reject the touch, either.

"Whenever Henry found us, he said it was my fault that he couldn't let go. Sometimes I thought I should give in. So many times I almost did. But the kids wouldn't let me. They were my strength. They shouldn't have had to be, but they were." Karen paused to wipe a tear from her cheek, but another took its place. They streamed down her face, coming faster than ever, and the sight horrified Bailey more than anything she'd heard so far. Because it meant that somehow, something worse was coming.

"The last time Henry found us, we were doing well. It had been four years since we'd left, and a couple of years since we'd last seen him; I actually let myself hope that he'd given up. I'd gotten a job and we had a little flat. Cash was at school again, and Monroe was working part-time at the supermarket. And it was… it was good. It was perfect.

"But then he came. I was at work, and so was Monroe—only Cash was at home." Karen sobbed, the sound raw and anguished. She buried her face in her hands and Bailey rubbed soothing circles over her shaking back.

After a moment, Karen regained control. She wiped the tears from her face, taking off her glasses and letting them hang from their little chain around her neck. "Cash never told me what happened. I had to read it in the police report. Henry broke in and he… he tried to kill Cash. With a knife! He stabbed my boy! The woman next door heard the commotion and called the police. They were both arrested. I had to tell the police everything. I knew from experience, they don't listen to women like me. But I had to *make* them listen.

"Well, I needn't have worried. You see, Henry'd left us alone for so long because he found someone else. A young girl—her name was Summer. I suppose he thought she'd be easy to control, like me. He miscalculated. A few weeks before he found us, he'd lost his temper and beaten her bloody over some small thing—I don't know. She was talking to the postman, I think, and Henry said she was making a fool of herself. Embarrassing him. So they argued, and he beat her, and she went straight to the police and showed them everything." Karen gave a little smile, and Bailey understood. The smile was for Summer. For the girl who'd done what Karen couldn't.

"Henry resisted arrest and disappeared—I suppose that's when he came after us. So the police listened. They questioned Cash and they interviewed Monroe and me. Henry was charged with all sorts—domestic violence, grievous bodily harm, assault with intent to resist arrest, perverting the course of justice, breaking and entering, attempted murder." She reeled off the charges from memory, her words taking on a clipped precision.

"They gave him a life sentence; twenty-five years before parole. I near-fainted when they found him guilty."

At the knowledge that, on this rare occasion, justice had prevailed, Bailey felt a bit faint herself. So many stories like Karen's were never-ending—or worse. And the scars of this family's experience would always be there.

But at least, God willing, there'd be no more.

"I don't tell you this for—for sympathy. Not at all. It sounds so dramatic when you tell the story all at once!" Karen laughed softly. "But when you live it, it's very slow. And fear becomes mundane. You grow immune. It's like waking up early for work; at first it's a struggle, but eventually you find yourself up with the sunrise on a Sunday. You become accustomed.

"The thing is, Cash was always very sensitive. He never became accustomed. He never got numb like me. He had counselling, both my kids did—I made sure. But I realised, over the years, that he was pushing people away; avoiding anything close to love. Rejecting affection. I nearly expired on the spot when he said he was bringing you home. He is twenty-nine years old and he has *never* introduced me to a woman. Not ever." Bailey shifted uncomfortably against the mattress. The past month flashed through her mind in fractured pieces, like a puzzle that was starting to come together. And the final image... It just might break her heart.

"When he feels things—*anything*—too strongly, Cash will push that thing away. Even his career; when he first became successful, he almost sabotaged everything. It was as though he felt he didn't deserve it, or that he was doomed to ruin it somehow." Karen nibbled at her lip nervously. "Do you understand what I'm saying, Bailey?"

"I... I think I do." Bailey let the horrors she'd just heard sink into her mind. Her first instinct was to reject them utterly, to listen with a shallow ear, to let the words wash over her like an advertisement on the radio. Her brain begged to travel elsewhere, railed against the harsh realities forced onto it in the last fifteen minutes.

But she could not allow that. Karen had just spilled her own blood across the carpet; basic respect demanded that Bailey truly bear witness. Her mother had always said that one thing *everyone* could do to ease another's pain was to acknowledge it. Bailey put her hand over Karen's and let their eyes meet, brown capturing blue. "I do understand," she said. "And I thank you. And I'm sorry."

"Well… alright then." Karen patted Bailey's hand in turn. Then she stood up and tugged at her own apron strings, as though her hands needed something to do. After one last look around the room, she walked towards the door.

"Karen," Bailey said. "I don't suppose you know where Cash has gone?"

With a small, hopeful smile, Karen turned back. "Probably. He often goes to the old church, past the woods. Helps him think. If you wait a little while, he should be back soon. He's never gone for long."

"Okay," Bailey said. "Thanks."

She waited just long enough for Karen to bustle off downstairs. And then she got up and pulled her hat and scarf out of her bag.

Waiting had never been her thing.

CHAPTER 23

The lavender sky plunged into darkness like a pearl into midnight waters. Cash watched the moon grow brighter against its dimming backdrop, barely noticing the whip of the icy wind against his cheeks.

He deserved the discomfort, just as he deserved every part of the aching numbness that had infected his blood. He knew that much.

The hulking carcass of the old church loomed before him, the wind whistling through the jagged remains of its stained glass windows. He gazed up at the imposing arcs and spears of its silhouette, but for the first time, he wasn't inspired. His fingers didn't itch to pick up a pen. Which was just as well, because he hadn't brought his sketchbook and his hands were frozen stiff.

Another pain that he deserved.

Furious with himself, Cash turned his back on the gothic beauty that had always soothed him. He'd been a fool to think that the usual tactics would work. There was nothing usual about this situation.

There was nothing usual about the woman he'd left behind, or the way she made him feel.

"I'm not in love with Bailey."

"I'm a fucking liar," he muttered to himself. The wind snatched away his words. He liked that; it made him feel braver. "I'm a liar," he repeated. "And a coward. I—"

He broke off. There was a figure approaching, wandering out from the trees with a halting gait. A figure he recognised.

But she was… limping?

Cash ran across the frosted grass, his boots kicking up icy chunks of dirt. He reached her in moments, pulled her into his arms as though he hadn't seen her in weeks.

But she was stiff, cold in more ways than one. Of course she was. God, where the fuck was his sense?

He pulled back, looked down into her face and found fury. That was to be expected. But there was something else there, something that broke his heart. Pain gleamed like a knife's edge in her soft, brown eyes.

"You're hurt," he said.

"Don't touch me."

"Bailey—"

"I mean it."

Cash took a deep breath. Let her go. Stepped back. And then he tried again. "You're hurt. What's wrong with your leg?"

"I fell," she said shortly. "Landed on my knee."

"What are you doing out here?"

"Looking for you."

As though he wasn't guilty enough. "We need to get you home. I can carry you."

"Where the fuck do you get off, acting like you give a shit?"

That felt like a slap. He wanted to do something to stop this—to stop the pain of the best thing he'd never had splintering before his eyes—but he shouldn't. He wouldn't.

He. Deserved. This.

"Well?" she demanded.

"The cold will make it worse." He began walking back towards the house, hoping she would follow. But she didn't, of course.

"Why do you care?" she shouted at his back, accusation crawling over her words.

He looked back at her and wondered if she could see his heart shattering through his chest. "You think I don't care about you, Bailey? You're wrong. I care about you so much, it worries me."

"Then stop the bullshit, Cash. Stop the hot and cold, stop with the *mystery* and just fucking—just *talk* to me! Now. *Right* now."

She made it sound so simple. As though *talking*—telling her exactly what a mess he was—would make things better instead of worse. His first instinct was to push her away somehow, to take the choice out of both their hands.

But something about the way she was looking at him spoke of finality. Of the fact that this might be his last chance. At what, he didn't know; but the thought of wasting it terrified him more than any of his demons ever could.

Then she said, "Your mother talked to me."

BAILEY WATCHED as Cash turned away, running a hand through his hair. In the swelling shadows, he seemed to mirror the imposing silhouette of the church that stood behind him, piercing the sky. He turned back to her with a haunted, hopeless expression that didn't belong on a man like him, a man who moved mountains. She wanted to replace that look with something else, something warm and contented, forever. But she couldn't.

That was up to him.

"What did she tell you?" he asked, his voice ragged.

"Well," she said, gently. "I think I know now, how you got that scar." Her voice, so bold moments ago, was soft. Hesitant.

He laughed, but the sound was harsh. "I want to piss you off," he said. "I want you furious again, to burn away the pity."

"I've never pitied you and I never will." She stood firm, watched as he studied her face. As he saw the truth in her eyes.

His gaze shuttered. “Bailey. You must know by now that I’m not the kind of man you can be with.”

“Why? Because of your past?” She shook her head. “If you’re afraid—I understand that. But I want to help.”

He shook his head, a sharp smile twisting his face. “Is that what you think? That I’m scared for myself?”

“Aren’t you?”

“No. I’m scared for *you*, Bailey. Do you realise what a fuck-up I am? Do you realise that—that if I’m not careful, I’ll end up just like him?”

“Why would you say that?” she asked, horrified. A tear ran down her cheek, tracing fire across the icy plane of her skin.

His arrogant veneer crumbled when he saw her cry. He came to her, swiped the tear away with a thumb; then he cupped her face tenderly, as though she were something precious. She allowed herself to be swept away by the sensation, until he spoke again, his voice solemn.

“There’s a beast inside of me. I keep it caged. You drive it wild.”

Confusion pleating her brow, she peered up at him. “So are you, like, a werewolf?”

He squinted. “…No, Bailey. I’m not a werewolf.” Then he laughed. The sound was weak, broken, but real—and despite the icy chill, her heart grew warm. He bumped his forehead against hers, and some of the strain was gone from his features. “A werewolf? Really? You’re so fucking cute.”

“Shut up,” she huffed. “It’s not my fault you decided to be all dramatic.” But she was smiling, because even when she fucking furious and confused and upset, Cash could always make her smile.

His face returned to solemnity, and he shook his head. “I’m not being dramatic. I’m a mess, Bailey. And it never really mattered before, because I had nobody to inflict it on. But I can’t hide it from you. And I can’t give you anything better.”

She studied his face, saw honesty there. But she just didn't *understand*.

"Why do you think that?" she asked softly. "Tell me."

He hesitated. When he spoke, the words were wincing and hesitant, as though they didn't often see the light of day. "I have… thoughts. Intrusive thoughts. I bet you know what that means."

"I do." Unwelcome, involuntary thoughts that were difficult to manage or ignore; sometimes associated with mental illness; sometimes the result of trauma. In his case, probably the latter, or both. "What do you see?" she asked.

"Hear. I hear it."

"Okay," she said slowly. "So you have these thoughts. And they make you think that you're… that you're like your father?"

He shook his head. "They *tell* me I'm like him. No matter what I do—they tell me that I'll end up hurting people. Like he hurt…" His voice trailed off and he squeezed his eyes shut, his expression fierce. He probably looked intimidating to most people. Terrifying, even. He was a big guy; he was tatted; he stomped around in those fucking boots and all that leather, and when he wasn't smiling he looked something close to feral.

But Bailey had never been scared of this man. Not once. Because she knew who he really was.

"Cash," she said gently. "I'm not afraid of you."

He opened his eyes. "I know. And I want to keep it that way."

"I will *never* be afraid of you. Intrusive thoughts can't tell you who you are. Only you decide that. If you need to push people away to feel safe, I understand. But pushing people away for *their* safety is a different thing entirely. I am a grown woman. If I want to love an accountant from a neat little family who goes fishing on Sundays, I will. And if I want to love *you*, Cash, I will. You can't stop love. All you can do is take it or reject it."

He stared down at her with something perilously close to hope, something so vulnerable that it made her heart ache. But then his gaze shifted once more, and she felt him pulling back into self-doubt.

"You don't understand," he said stiffly. "I'm just like him. I… I tried to kill him, the day he came for us. I would have, if the police hadn't arrived." A tear slid down his own cheek, and the sight almost broke her. His voice was shaky as he continued. "I said it was self-defence. It wasn't. I saw him before I saw the knife and I decided right then that I would kill him. I just wanted my family to be safe, and I couldn't think of any other way—fuck, I didn't *think*. I didn't weigh up the pros and cons. Morals didn't come into it. I saw him and I wanted him dead." He took a ragged breath. "That's the kind of person I am, Bailey."

She reached up and slid her hands into his hair, angled his head until he was forced to look down and meet her eyes.

"There's nothing wrong with wanting to protect your family. Defending the ones you love isn't twisted or cruel. Can you imagine your father doing something like that? Knowing he'd spend the rest of his life locked away, without the ones he'd sacrificed for?"

Cash shook his head. "I didn't need to be with them. I just needed to know they'd be safe."

"Exactly." She rose up on her toes, pressing her forehead to his. "Your love is as fierce as you are, Cash. That's all."

His eyes were wide, hungry, desperate. He wrapped his arms around her waist, held her as though she might disappear at any moment. "God, I want to believe you. The way you make me feel…"

"How *do* I make you feel?"

"When I saw you for the first time, I felt like… Fuck, I felt like I'd been punched in the face." He choked out a laugh. "I felt like my life would be a failure if I never got to know you. And then I worried that I was building you up too much in my head. But I wasn't. You're more than I ever dreamed you would be. We met two months ago, Bailey. *Two months*. And I would kill for you. That's not normal."

"Doesn't have to be normal to be right," she murmured. "Cash, I never wanted to be with anyone. Not really. All I've ever seen of love is the way it drains people; the way it uses them up and leaves them wanting. I grew up thinking of love as a vampire. And I was always left to nurse my mother back to health when it attacked.

"I never understood how she fell so hard every time. But I'm starting to. If loving someone feels like this… I'm starting to. And I know now why they call it *falling*. You can't just step into this shit. And you can't stop it once it's started. You have to be brave. You have to believe that someone's going to catch you."

Around them, the temperature sank lower as night crept over the grass. The huge, old church behind him was just a terrifying shadow now, any semblance of beauty blanked out by the bone-white glare of the moon. But between them, the air was hot. His warm breath soothed her wind-chapped cheeks; his hands on her were so delicious, she almost forgot the ache in her knee. And his gaze was burning like the fire in the home they'd left behind.

"You know that I'd catch you," he said. "Don't you?"

"Of course I do," she whispered, and as she said the words, she realised they were true. They really were. The knowledge rang through her body like the sound of shattered glass.

No—of shattered ice.

She wasn't afraid anymore.

But it was no good being brave alone.

"Do *you* know it, Cash?"

"I trust you," he told her.

"I believe you. But that's not all it takes. You have to trust yourself."

He cursed softly, and all of a sudden he was gone. The shelter his big body provided was cruelly stolen, and cold swept in with a vengeance. He paced away from her, raking his hands through his hair, muttering to himself. The traitorous wind carried the sound to her ears—just enough for her to hear the frustration in his tone. Not enough to make out the words.

Hot tears spilled down her cheeks, and she let them. It didn't matter, now. A thought pushed its way to the front of her mind, refusing to leave, even though she knew better. *Nothing matters now*, it whispered. *Nothing.*

She turned and limped away.

"Bailey!" He was back within seconds, sweeping her up into his arms. "What are you doing? You aren't walking on that knee."

She wanted to tell him to put her down, to get off of her, to disappear completely so she might have some chance of ever feeling whole again. But she didn't even know if that would work, or if it would only ruin her further. And anyway, when she tried to speak, all that came out was a garbled sob.

"Don't cry," he said, horrified. "Bailey! Please don't cry." And then she felt his lips tracing their way across her cheeks, making constellations of her teardrops. His thick stubble tickled her skin, somehow comforting and devastating all at once.

"Bailey," he whispered. "Sweetheart. I know I hurt you. I know I'm… God, I'm a bastard. I know that. But I want to be better and I want to be braver and it's all because of you."

Wait. This was not what she'd been ready to hear. And maybe it was foolish, but her hopeful heart sat up and listened.

"I want to be the one who cares for you. I want to be the one who makes you smile. I want to be the man you spend every Christmas with. I want to love you the way you deserve to be loved." He took a breath. Cradled against his broad chest, she felt the air shudder through his lungs. "I do love you, Bailey. And I know I don't deserve it, but if you could give me a chance—"

He was forced into silence when she pressed her mouth to his. Her kiss was clumsy, frenzied, desperate. All the things she'd never wanted to be. And yet, when he kissed her back with just as much fervour, she found she didn't mind it at all.

"Is that a yes?" he panted against her lips.

"What are you asking?"

"Be mine. For more than ninety days. For as long as you'll have me."

Bailey tangled her gloved fingers through his hair and said, "Forever, then?"

"Yes," he whispered, and his piercing gaze became achingly tender. "Forever."

She dragged his head down and kissed him again.

IT HAD TAKEN Karen almost an hour to notice that Bailey was missing. Now she paced in the living room with an anxious Monroe, cursing and panicking at as high a volume as she'd ever managed. Clearly, it was up to George to be the group's calming presence.

"I bet she's fine," Monroe said in her lying-for-your-own-good voice.

"But are you *sure*?" demanded Karen, twisting her apron with reddened fingers.

"Yes," Monroe said firmly, still obviously lying.

"She doesn't know this area," George interjected. "And she might fall into a ditch and twist her ankle and freeze to death. And then there will be police at the house on Christmas morning, and the boys will have very bad memories."

Monroe looked at him in blank astonishment. So very pretty, was his wife. Karen wailed and began pacing with renewed energy.

"Now, what would you say that for?!" Monroe finally demanded.

"It's a genuine concern," George said. "I think I should go and look for her."

"Shut up!" Karen interrupted, flapping her hands. She ran to the window, peering out past the flashing Christmas lights. "Shut up, shut up, shut up! I'm trying to see."

"Mother," Monroe sighed. "I don't think your hearing and your sight are connected."

"Oh, no, they definitely are," George countered sagely. "I'm quite sure of it." He moved to look over Karen's shoulder.

"I think I see them!" she was shrieking. He squinted into the darkness, watched a growing shape in the distance come closer. Within seconds, it was almost identifiable. "Yes," Karen cried, her despair vanishing like smoke. "They're back! Oh, they're back! And—goodness me."

Monroe rushed to the window, pushing in front of him. He slipped an arm around her waist, taking a moment to enjoy the happiness on her lovely face. He was almost completely distracted by the sweet curls springing loose from her serviceable bun—but then he remembered that he was supposed to be watching the window.

So he looked again, and saw Cash clearly now, walking towards the house with Bailey in his arms. He was looking down at her with an expression that George had never seen on the man's face before. And Bailey, for her part, was looking up at Cash with an equally baffling smile. It was soft and silly and vaguely familiar. It took George a second to place it, but eventually he did.

That was how Monroe looked at him—when he wasn't making her growl with frustration. And sometimes, when he was.

Well, then. It seemed they'd all have a very merry Christmas after all.

EPILOGUE

FIVE YEARS LATER

It was the night before Christmas, and all through the house, not a soul was stirring.

Except for Cooper Evans, of course.

"I'll get him!" Karen cried, jumping up from her seat at the kitchen island. Cooper had been put to bed hours earlier, but now his cries rang out from the baby monitor on the counter.

"Are you sure?" Cash asked. "I can get him."

"No, no. You keep Bailey company. I'll sort him out." Karen bustled off out of the room, leaving Cash and Bailey alone in the kitchen.

Theirs was a big family now. Someone could walk in at any moment. Which, in Cash's mind, meant he'd better go and pester his wife quickly, before anyone came to interrupt.

She stood with her back to him, slicing up vegetables for tomorrow as though nothing was amiss. But he knew this woman. The set of her shoulders, the angle of those lush hips, told him that she was waiting. Waiting, probably with a smile on her sweet lips, for his touch.

Well, he wouldn't want to disappoint her, now, would he?

Crossing the tiled floor in a few short strides, Cash slid his arms around his wife's waist, resting his hands on the swell of life that was her rounded belly. He pressed his lips to the soft skin of her neck, smiling as she lay down her knife and sank into him.

"Hello, Doctor Evans," he murmured.

"Not yet," she said softly. "Don't jinx me." But there was laughter in her voice.

"You know it's in the bag. Just like your Master's was." He rubbed his palm over her stomach, cradled the precious bump. Kissed her neck, then bit gently as she arched into him.

Karen's voice came through the monitor, strident as always. "Cooper!" She was cooing. "Shhh, now."

"No!" The toddler cried, loud enough to rival his grandmother. "Want *Daddy*!"

"Your son calls," Bailey chuckled.

Cash rolled his eyes. "With any luck, this next one will attach herself to you." But his smile was wide and his heart was full. Cash was his son's favourite person in the world. It made him positively faint with pride.

And with gratitude. Bailey had given him this. Bailey had given him love.

"I believe she'll be a daddy's girl, actually," his wife called after him. "Then you'll have another shadow to trail your every move."

Cash shook his head fondly as he left the kitchen, Bailey's laughter chasing after him.

He came across John's daughters on the stairs, playing a game that involved decapitated Bratz dolls and, it seemed, tragic falls to the death. Cash watched as one doll pushed another savagely down the steps, cackling her triumph in a little girl's voice.

"Shouldn't you girls be in bed?" he asked finally. The eldest, Magda, paused her doll's vengeful monologue to give him a pitying look.

"No, Uncle Cash. I'm ten now, remember?"

He looked at the younger girl, Alice. She avoided his gaze. "And what about your sister?" he pushed.

"Um…"

"To bed. Or I'll tell your fathers."

"Uncle Cash!" Their voices rang out in unison. Four eyes—one pair blue, one pair dark as ink—turned on him in frustration.

"Take Alice back to bed, Mags. You know the rules."

"Ugh!" Magda cried. But she collected the dolls, along with her six-year-old sister, and they stormed off to their shared room.

Cash continued up the stairs, then ascended the next flight. There he found John, leaning against the bannister with a smirk.

"You knew they were up?" Cash asked.

"Just noticed. But it's so much easier to let *you* get on their bad side."

Cash rolled his eyes. "Did Pete know you were such a pushover when he agreed to the whole parenting thing?"

"Of course not. It's my most closely-guarded secret."

Cash chuckled as he left his friend behind, single-minded in his quest to reach Cooper. From the moment John had met his little girls, he'd become a soft, mushy pudding of a man. But then again, Cash thought as he pushed open the door to his son's room, John wasn't the only one.

"Hey, little man," Cash murmured, rushing forward to relieve his mother of her snotty, crying load. "What's up with you?" He cradled the two-year-old in his arms, and the boy's sobbing instantly slowed.

"I don't know why I bother," Karen griped. But there was a tender smile on her face.

Cash bent down to kiss her soft cheek. "Thanks, Mum."

"Of course, my darling. Oh, I do love having you all here." A tear slid down her face, and she wiped it away impatiently. "All the children. We've so many now! And George and Monroe, and John and Pete, and—" Her voice cracked, but she soldiered on. "And you and Bailey! Oh, Cashew Nut, I'm so proud of you."

His face heating up, Cash pulled his mother into a hug. Cooper, now babbling contentedly to himself, patted her head with his clumsy, chubby palm. "Ganma!" he beamed, snot still bubbling from his nose. "Love Ganma."

She chuckled through her tears, kissing the toddler's damp face. "I love you too, little muffin."

And Cash pressed a kiss to his mother's ginger head, and then to his son's dark curls. Contentment washed over him, bright and pure as the moonlight. In this small room, silence reigned, and he allowed himself to enjoy it. There were no whispers to threaten his fulfilment; no uninvited thoughts taking up space inside his mind. Some days there would be, sure—but when those days came, he had someone to face them with. Someone to hold his hand and chase away his fear. Someone to love him anyway.

Cash held his mother and his son in his arms, filled with gratitude. Around them, the house sank into the quiet excitement of Christmas Eve like a baby sinks into a crib.

A house that was full of the very love he thought he'd never have.

DOWNSTAIRS, the woman who'd given it to him sat at the kitchen island, holding the baby monitor with a smile on her face. She pressed a palm to her swollen stomach—

And beneath her hand, their daughter kicked.

"Patience, sweetheart," Bailey murmured. "Next year, you'll be here to join in."

The baby kicked again, as though expressing her eagerness. Bailey smiled as she felt tiny feet pressing against her, a firm declaration: *I am here, and I won't be ignored!* This child took after her grandmother, it seemed.

Both grandmothers.

The thought of her mother no longer disturbed Bailey's equilibrium. Instead of resentment, she thought only of fond memories; of Dorothy applying her own ruby-red lipstick to Bailey's little face; of the two of them watching Disney films on a Sunday night, throwing popcorn at each other when the other wasn't looking.

She rose from her seat and went back to the chopping board with a smile on her face. As she sliced up carrots and parsnips for the next day's feast, Bailey reflected on the miracle Cash had brought into her life.

Peace.

The very best gift of all.

AUTHOR'S NOTE

Homelessness in Britain is on the rise, and certain groups are especially vulnerable. From LGBTQ+ youth to victims of domestic violence, the disadvantaged are often the first to suffer.

This Christmas, whether you choose to celebrate or not, I ask that you bear in mind the principles of love and kindness to all. Everyone is human; everyone deserves safety. No matter where you live, someone in your local community needs you—even if all you have to give is friendship.

And if you find yourself in need, remember that your circumstances do not diminish your humanity.

Merry Christmas, everyone. Thanks for reading.

Talia x

ABOUT THE AUTHOR

Talia Hibbert is a *New York Times, USA Today,* and *Wall Street Journal* bestselling author who lives in a bedroom full of books. Supposedly, there is a world beyond that room—but she has yet to drum up enough interest to investigate.

She writes steamy, diverse romance because she believes that people of marginalised identities need honest and positive representation. She also rambles intermittently about the romance genre over at Frolic Media. Her interests include makeup, junk food, and unnecessary sarcasm.

And, as Talia would say... that's all, folks. Love and biscuits!

https://www.taliahibbert.com

Made in United States
Troutdale, OR
12/03/2025